Helen Paiba was one of the most committed, knowledgeable and acclaimed children's booksellers in Britain. For more than twenty years she owned and ran the Children's Bookshop in Muswell Hill, London, which under her guidance gained a superb reputation for its range of children's books and for the advice available to its customers.

Helen was also involved with the Booksellers Association for many years and served on both its Children's Bookselling Group and the Trade Practices Committee.

In 1995 she was given honorary life membership of the Booksellers Association of Great Britain and Ireland in recognition of her outstanding services to the association and to the book trade. In the same year the Children's Book Circle (sponsored by Books for Children) honoured her with the Eleanor Farjeon Award, given for distinguished service to the world of children's books.

Books in this series

Funny Stories for 5 Year Olds

Funny Stories for 6 Year Olds

Funny Stories for 7 Year Olds

Funny Stories for 8 Year Olds

Magical Stories for 5 Year Olds

Magical Stories for 6 Year Olds

Scary Stories for 7 Year Olds

Scary stories

for 7 Year Olds

Chosen by Helen Paiba

Illustrated by Kerstin Meyer

MACMILLAN CHILDREN'S BOOKS

For Ann and David
H.P.

First published 1998 by Macmillan Children's Books

This edition published 2016 by Macmillan Children's Books
an imprint of Pan Macmillan
20 New Wharf Road, London N1 9RR
Associated companies throughout the world
www.panmacmillan.com

ISBN 978-1-5098-1832-7

3 5 7 9 8 6 4

A CIP catalogue record for this book is available from
the British Library.

Typeset by SX Composing DTP, Rayleigh, Essex
Printed and bound by CPI Group (UK) Ltd, Croydon CR0 4YY

Contents

The Haunted Suitcase

Colin Thompson

Under the roof of the house, below dark beams carved from the ribs of ancient sailing ships, was the attic. Hardly anyone ever went up there. It was a calm quiet place where the air stood still and the sounds from the rooms below were muffled by a heavy layer of dust. A thin wash of sunshine came in through a single skylight, throwing a million shadows around all the junk stored there. Boxes of books and old photographs, and chests full of ancient memories filled the place. In the darkest corners there were crumbling trunks that had stood there for hundreds of years. And in those time-worn containers, in soft paper-lined tunnels lived the most horrendous spiders you could

1

imagine. They had been there so long that they had evolved into a unique species, a species that, because they had eaten nothing but books for hundreds of generations, had developed into a race of super-intelligent beings.

Because of the spiders, there were no ghosts in the attic. Even the most ferocious ghost was too frightened to live there. And even the most stupid ghost was not so stupid that he didn't shake with fear at the thought of them. All except one ghost, and it had no choice. Unable to move by any means, flight, telepathy or plain walking, it sat in the middle of the floor, terrified out of its tiny mind. It shone in the moonlight, a dull brown glow of antique leather. Nothing went near it, not even the dust. It was the haunted suitcase.

It was forty years since the last person had been up into the attic. The suitcase had been there then. It gave off an uneasy feeling that made people keep away from it. Sixty years before someone had put a box of old magazines up there. The suitcase had been there then too. And in 1890, when the housekeeper had been up looking for a lost maid, the suitcase had definitely been there.

"Can we go up in the attic and play?" asked Alice one morning at breakfast.

"I suppose so," said her mother.

"Who's *we*?" asked Peter.

"You and me," said Alice.

"No way," said Peter. "I'm not going up there. It's much too dangerous."

"Who says?" said Alice. "I've never heard a single sound from up there."

"Exactly," said Peter.

"There's dark forces up there," said Peter's granny ominously.

"See," said Alice. "Dark forces. I told you there was nothing to worry about."

Two sprites started chasing each other through everyone's breakfast, splashing milk everywhere, so the attic was forgotten while they tried to get them back into the cereal box.

"If you don't let us out," they shouted through the cardboard, "you'll be sorry."

"Oh yes," said Alice. "What will you do?"

"We'll destroy all the cornflakes," said the first sprite.

"And the plastic toy," said the second.

"Yeah," said the first. "We're cereal killers."

By the time they'd wiped the table with the ghost of a witch's cat and finished their breakfast everyone was talking about something else. But at lunchtime Peter's father said, "You know it's funny you should mention the attic. I've been thinking we should clear it out."

"Best let sleeping dogs lie," said Peter's granny.

"Are there dogs up there as well?" asked Alice. "Let's go up please, please."

"It'll end in tears," said Peter's granny.

But after lunch they got a ladder, and Peter's father opened the trapdoor, climbed into the loft and disappeared.

For a long time there was complete silence. Peter and Alice stood at the bottom of the ladder looking up into the dark square in the ceiling.

"Dad," said Alice, "can we come up?"

"I think we should stay here and hold the ladder," said Peter.

"You're just a big baby," said Alice and climbed up after her father. Once again there was complete silence.

"Dad, Alice," said Peter, "is everything all right?"

There were shuffling noises coming from the loft and a thick cloud of dust crawling out of the trapdoor. Peter put his hand over his nose, took a deep breath and climbed up the ladder.

There were so many old boxes and dust everywhere it was a bit like being a giant in a foggy city. Peter's dad and Alice were over in the far corner opening boxes and pulling things out left, right and centre.

"Can you go and get a torch?" asked Peter's dad. "This place is a treasure trove."

And so it was. Over the next few weeks, they unearthed old books and vases worth a small fortune. It was like a hundred Christmases all at once. The vile spiders moved back deeper and deeper into the darkest corners until there was almost nowhere left for them to go. The haunted suitcase sat by the water tank and waited. For some strange reason neither Peter nor Alice nor their dad seemed to have noticed it.

"It'll end in tears," said Peter's granny. "You mark my words."

After six weeks, the attic was almost empty. Six crumbling boxes, too old to move, lay along the farthest wall, and inside them the spiders sat and waited. For the first time in three hundred years, they were frightened. It was a strange, exciting feeling but none of them knew how to handle it. Ghosts and ghouls they could deal with, but humans, especially small girls who looked like they might eat spiders, they were something different.

"Maybe we should rush out and terrorize them," said the oldest spider, Eddie.

"Yeah," said his sister Edna, "if all the ghosts are scared of us, a few humans'd be easy."

"I don't know," said Eddie's brother, Eric. "There are three of them."

"Yeah," said Eddie, "but there are three thousand nine hundred and seventy-two of us."

"Three thousand nine hundred and seventy-one," said Edna. "I've just eaten young Eamon."

"I'm not sure about that girl," said Eddie. "She looks like she could eat all of us in one go."

"Come on," said Edna. "We're the most ferocious spiders in the world."

"Of course we are," said Eddie. "Let's go."

So on the count of seven they all ran out. As they raced across the floor they suddenly heard a dreadful ear-shattering roar.

"I wonder why all spiders have names beginning with 'e'," thought Edna as the roar came closer and closer. For centuries the spiders had lived in the attic. They had heard ten thousand thunderstorms and the bombs of several wars but that had all been outside. This noise was inside, right there all around them and it was the loudest thing they had ever heard.

"Oh, look," said Alice, as she vacuumed the

ancient Chinese carpet that covered the attic floor, "hundreds of tiny weeny spiders."

They may have frightened ghosts and they may have thought they were the most ferocious spiders in the world, but because they had lived alone for so long they had forgotten that they were also some of the smallest spiders in the world, so small that Alice could hardly see them.

"Hello, tiny spiders," she said. "Come and play inside the vacuum cleaner."

The last of the dust and old boxes was cleared away and it was only then that someone noticed the haunted suitcase. Peter had spent all morning cleaning and polishing and he was exhausted. He sat on the old suitcase and closed his eyes.

"Where did that come from?" said Alice.

"What?" said Peter.

"That suitcase."

"That's odd," said their dad. "I wonder why we never noticed it."

"It was probably hidden under the water tank," said Peter. But it hadn't been. It had actually been moving slowly around the attic, hoping someone would notice it.

"I wonder what's inside," said Alice.

They tried to open it, but the suitcase didn't want to be opened in the attic. It wanted to be downstairs in the warm sunshine. It had been cold for far too long.

"It's locked," said Peter.

"We'll take it down to the kitchen and open it there," said Peter's dad.

"Yeah!" thought the suitcase.

They cleared the kitchen table and put the suitcase in the middle. It wasn't very big or heavy, no bigger than a small box, really.

"Come on, come on," said Alice, "bash the locks off."

As soon as the suitcase heard that, it sprung its locks and began shivering. The few ghosts that were awake ran out into the garden and Peter's granny went to the lavatory. "I think this is where it ends in tears," she said.

Peter lifted the lid and as he did so a few socks fell out.

"It's just full of old clothes," he said and it was, full of socks, millions and millions and millions of them.

They poured out of the suitcase like oil from an oil well. They covered the table and piled up on the floor until everyone was ankle deep in them.

"Shut it," shouted Peter's mum, but no one could. They dragged the case into the garage and locked the doors and still the socks kept pouring out.

By next morning they had reached the roof

and were packing themselves in tighter and tighter until the doors were straining at their hinges.

"I wish I'd taken the car out first," said Peter's dad.

They collected up all the socks from the kitchen, three thousand and twenty-seven of them. And every single one was different. Inside the haunted suitcase were all the odd socks that everyone in the world had ever lost.

"Maybe there's another suitcase somewhere with all the other ones in," suggested Peter, but there wasn't, because the sock that got left behind was always used as a duster or a rag to clean up after a new puppy.

On Tuesday, the garage doors collapsed and the socks began to pour out into the garden. On Wednesday, Peter's Aunt Sophie, who was staying for the weekend, said she would take the suitcase. She had an idea.

She tunnelled into the garage and carried the suitcase out to a large truck. Their poor car had sock dents all over it and for months they kept finding socks in the most unlikely places. They turned up in parts of the house where the suitcase hadn't even been. The strangest one was on Christmas day when they found a very old worn-out sock in the middle of the Christmas pudding.

Aunt Sophie drove the truck into the middle of a massive factory and twenty-four hours a day forever after, two hundred people sorted the socks into pairs. Because, although they were all odd socks, there are only so many different possible types of sock. So if you lost a green one with orange spots in a cottage in Scotland, someone, somewhere else in the world would, one day, be bound to lose a sock exactly the same as yours.

"It'll end in tears," said Peter's granny, who had been put in charge of everyone in the sock factory.

"No, no," said Aunt Sophie. "It'll end in pairs."

Aunt Sophie opened a shop that just sold socks. Then she opened another one and another one until she had shops all over the world. And every day thousands of people bought new socks to replace the odd ones they had lost. Sometimes they probably bought back one of the very socks they had lost. There was even a man in Tasmania who bought his own lost socks back three times and never realized. He just thought how wonderful it was that they kept making the same pattern over and over again. And of course every day people kept on losing socks so the haunted suitcase was never empty.

The haunted suitcase sat in the middle of its huge factory, happier than it had ever been. Every day someone dusted it and stroked its brown leather skin with soft gentle polish that hadn't been tested on any animals at all and was full of wonderful things like marigolds and honey. Everyone loved the haunted suitcase because it had made them all very, very rich. Even Peter's granny finally admitted that it probably wouldn't end in tears after all.

I'm Scared!

. . . of the dark

Bel Mooney

"I'm not scared of anything – not me!" said Kitty, folding her arms, and standing by the back door.

Outside the wind was moaning, and rain rattled on the kitchen window.

"Yes, you are," said Daniel.

"No, I'm not," said Kitty.

"Kitty thinks she's big and brave!" jeered her brother.

"I *know* I am," shouted Kitty.

"Go out into the garden then!" said Daniel, with a big grin. "Walk to the end of the garden and back, on your own!"

Kitty looked outside. It was dark. The only

light in the garden came from the kitchen window – all strange and yellowish in the rain.

Wooooo-woooo went the wind.

"It's only our old garden," said Kitty. "Who's afraid of that? It's not worth doing!"

"*Dark* out there!" teased Daniel.

Kitty gulped.

"I dare you," said Daniel.

"No – I don't want to," said Kitty.

"Kitty's scared! Scaredy-Kitty-Kat!" Daniel laughed and laughed.

Kitty couldn't bear it.

"I jolly well will – so there!"she yelled, and pulled open the back door. She had taken one step away from the door, when she heard Daniel turn the key in the lock. And to be really mean, he pulled down the blind at the window, so there was much less light streaming out.

It was dark. And cold. And rainy. And still the wind went on sighing – as if it was sad.

Without stopping to think, Kitty began to walk. The garden seemed very different in this strange half-light. The bushes looked big and black, like huge animals waiting to pounce. The wind made them rustle . . .

What was that? A lion? A tiger?

Kitty knew it was only the redcurrant bush and the flowering shrubs – but her heart began to thud, and she started to walk more quickly.

What was that? A dinosaur?

Kitty knew it was only the wheelbarrow, upside down with a few plastic plant-pots dumped higgledy-piggledy on it – but her mouth went dry, and she turned her walk into a skip.

The sky had a few streaks of light in it – pink and yellow – and the trees stood out very blackly. They seemed to wave their bare arms in the air, as if to say, "Go back!"

Kitty remembered all those lovely illustrations in children's books, where the old trees in the forest wore scary faces, and their roots and branches were like arms and legs, waiting to reach out . . .

She wished she hadn't thought of them. She didn't want to remember them. Because it was easy to look at these trees – the friendly trees they liked to climb in their own garden

– and know for sure that they had faces too.

And the faces weren't friendly. Not at all.

There was a small creaking noise as the swing Dad had made blew backwards and forwards, backwards and forwards – as if some invisible person was pushing it . . .

Kitty took a deep breath, and started to run. In the daytime their garden seemed quite small, really – just an ordinary garden with a hedge all around, bordering the neighbours' gardens. But now in the dark it seemed enormous, with vast shadowy corners in which anything could hide.

What made it worse was that William's house was in total darkness. She knew they had all gone to stay with his aunt and uncle, and wouldn't be back until tomorrow. So – there was no help there.

But help for what?

Kitty ran as fast as her little legs would carry her. At the end of the garden was the shed.

It was a nice garden shed, with a door in the middle and a window each side, like a little house.

She loved the way Mum and Dad hung the gardening tools neatly on the wall inside, and there was a bench with all sorts of interesting things on it – like balls of string and hammers and nails and tiny flowerpots. It was a good place to play. In the day.

But now it wasn't like a friendly little house. It could be a dark hut . . . in a scary story . . . lived in by a wicked witch. . . .

Kitty stopped before she reached it. She was panting now, and very chilly, with rain running down her face. "I'm *scared*," she whispered. "I'm scared of the d-d-dark." She wanted to cry.

Then she turned to run back to the house – and something surprising happened. Mum and Dad must have been in different rooms, because suddenly all the lights went on at once. Their home glowed, like a beacon.

As the blaze of light hit the garden, lighting up all the things Kitty had passed, she saw exactly what they were. The redcurrant bush. The flowering shrubs. The upside-down wheelbarrow. The nice old trees, one of them with the swing hanging from it.

The wind still sighed, and the bushes still rustled, but now they seemed to be friendly, telling Kitty that she should be inside.

Wooohooooo . . . gooooo hooooooome!

Home! With the bright lights, and the fire, and sausages and mash for supper, and Mum and Dad, and Mr Tubs the bear waiting upstairs.

Kitty ran forward – only this time she wasn't scared. Not a bit. She knew she had been silly, and she wanted her supper.

Funnily, it only took a minute or so to reach the back door. When she tried the handle, it was unlocked. She pushed open the door and went inside.

"KITTY!" cried Mum, looking at her wet jumper and hair.

"Where've you been?" asked Dad, "I can't believe you were so silly as to go out without a coat."

"And in the dark!" said Mum.

Kitty sat down, looking very calm. "I wasn't scared," she said.

Then she saw Daniel looking at her. He thought she was going to tell on him. He knew he'd get into trouble, because Dad couldn't stand silly dares. He was *scared*.

"Dan thought he'd dropped his pen," said Kitty, "and I went to look for it – because he was scared to go out."

Her brother opened his mouth like a fish, then closed it again. Kitty knew he wouldn't dare to tell the truth!

The Great White Cat

A Story from Scandinavia

Amabel Williams-Ellis

Once upon a time, far away in the north of Norway, there was a hunter and he caught a big white bear, alive, in a trap. It was such a fine young bear that he hadn't the heart to kill it, so he thought he would take it to the King of Denmark for a present. So he tamed it, and a very good bear it was.

Now, as bear and man plodded along on their long, long journey to the court of the King of Denmark, they came, just on Christmas Eve, to the Dovrafell. Now the Dovrafell is a bad sort of a place at any time of the year. It's a wild moor, all bog and heather and rock, with hardly a tree for shelter, and it's worst of all in the dark of winter, with the wind roaring and a sky full of snow. However, they hadn't gone far when the hunter thought he saw a light. As he got nearer he saw it must be a candle in a cottage window. Very glad he was to see it, in a wild place like that with the snow coming on.

The hunter knocked at the door and greeted the man of the house politely, and asked if he could get house-room there for his bear and himself.

"You might come and welcome," said the man, whose name was Halvor. "But deary me! We can't give anyone house-room, not just now!"

"But it's perishing cold out here in the Dovrafell," said the hunter.

"So it is," said Halvor, "and I'm sorry for you, but we have a bad time in this house at this time of the year. Every Christmas, for years now, such a pack of Trolls come down upon us that we are always forced to flit out of the house ourselves! Deary me! These seven years we haven't had so much as a house over our own heads – not at Christmas – and often not a morsel of food. It's very hard on the poor children, so it is!"

"Oh," said the hunter, "if that's all, you can very well let in me and my bear. We're not afraid of Trolls. My bear's a quiet fellow. He can lie under the stove yonder, and I can sleep in that little side-room you have by the kitchen."

Well, at first, Halvor said it would never do, but it was growing so cold outside, and the hunter begged so hard, that, at last, he and his bear were allowed to stay. So in they came. The bear lay down, and the hunter sat by the stove while the woman of the house began to get ready their Christmas dinner with the three children helping her. The hunter thought it was a queer sight to watch them getting the good things ready, for they had never a smile on their faces though they had managed to get together quite a nice feast, so that the hunter's mouth watered. But neither the good woman nor the children nor Halvor were very cheerful about it all, for, you see, they feared that it would only be the Trolls that would get it after all.

Next day was Christmas Day and, sure enough, no sooner had they all sat down to their Christmas dinner than down came the whole pack of Trolls. Some came down the chimney and some came through the windows. They all shouted and banged about and made such a hullabaloo that, in a fright, Halvor, his wife, and the three children got up from their places without having tasted a bite, and all ran to the woodshed and shut and locked the door. For you see Trolls are ill creatures and, if it had come to a fight, Halvor thought that the whole cottage might have been wrecked and the children hurt.

As for the hunter, he sat still in a corner, and watched to see what would happen. Some of the Trolls were big and some were little, and all were black and hairy. Some had long tails, and some had no tails at all, and some had noses as long as pokers. They all went on shouting and they put their feet and their tails on the table, threw the food about, and ate and drank, and messed and tasted everything. The little, screaming Trolls were the worst. They pulled each other's tails, fought over the food and even climbed up the curtains and began throwing such things as jars of jam and pickles, *smash*, off the kitchen shelves.

At last, one of these little Trolls caught sight of the great white bear, which all this time lay quiet and good under the stove. The little Troll found a piece of sausage and he stuck it on a fork.

"Pussy! Pussy! Will you have a bit of sausage?" he screamed as he poked the fork hard against the bear's tender black nose.

Then he laughed and pulled it away again so that the bear couldn't get the sausage.

Then the great white bear was very angry. Up he rose and, with a growl like thunder, he came out from under the stove and, in a moment, he had chased the whole pack of Trolls out of the house.

So the hunter praised him and patted him and gave him a big bit of sausage to eat in his place under the stove. Then he called Halvor and the family to come out of the woodshed. They were very surprised to find the Trolls gone, and they cleared up the mess while the hunter told them what had happened. Then they all sat down to eat what was left of their Christmas dinner.

The next day the hunter and the bear thanked Halvor and set out again on their long journey to the court of the King of Denmark.

Next year Halvor was out, just about sunset, in a wood at the edge of the Dovrafell on the afternoon of Christmas Eve. He was busy cutting all the wood they would want for the holiday. When he stopped to rest for a moment, leaning on his axe, he heard a voice that seemed to come from far away on the other side of the wood.

"Halvor! Halvor!" someone was shouting and calling.

"What do you want?" shouted Halvor. "Here I am."

"Have you got your big white cat with you still?" called the voice.

"Yes, that I have!" called back Halvor. "She's lying at home under the stove this moment. What's more, she has got seven kittens now, each bigger and fiercer than she is herself!"

"Then we'll never come to see you again!" bawled out the Troll from the other side of the wood.

What's more he never did, and so, since that time, the Trolls of the Dovrafell have never eaten their Christmas dinner at Halvor's house again.

Gobbleguts

Michael Rosen

Giant Gobbleguts lived in a cave and ate children. As soon as the children in the little village of No were big enough, Gobbleguts came raging down from the mountain, grabbed them, threw them into his Big Bad Bag and took them back to his cave. There he boiled them up in his great Stinking Stewing Pot and gobbled them down. He was truly horrible, and hairs grew out of his nose.

The last two children left in the village of No were twins.

"We're all alone," the two girls said to each other, "with no one to play with."

Flit and Flat, for those were their names, were still very, very small, but they knew that soon they would be big enough for Giant

Gobbleguts. And if *they* knew they were big enough, then you can be sure Giant Gobbleguts knew too.

"Let's not wait for him to come and get us," said Flit to Flat, "let's go and find him."

Up the mountain they walked, towards Giant Gobbleguts' cave. When they were nearly there, they came face to face with him and his horrible hairy nose.

"Who are you?" he roared.

"We're Flit and Flat and we were looking for you, Gobbleguts," said Flit and Flat.

"Oh were you?" Gobbleguts said, and he reached down and put them in the Big Bad Bag. Then he turned round and marched back towards his cave and the Stinking Stewing Pot.

"Now, here's my dinner for today," he said.

The girls took no notice and played foggy-plonks in the Big Bad Bag. About halfway to the cave, Flit hopped out of the Big Bad Bag and started throwing stones up to her sister.

When the Big Bad Bag was full, both girls jumped out and ran away off home.

Gobbleguts got back to his cave and lay down to rest.

"When I wake up I will have dinner. Oh yes, yes, yes. Lovely juicy children for dinner."

He slept and snored for a day or two. When he woke up, he opened the Big Bad Bag and all he found was a heap of stones. He thumped the walls of the cave and wailed, "Waaaaaaaaaaaaaaaaaaa, I've been tricked!"

A few days later, Giant Gobbleguts came out of his cave and marched down the mountain. Flit and Flat came out to meet him and his horrible hairy nose.

"Ah-hah. There you are, girls, I was looking for you."

"We were looking for you," said Flit and Flat.

Once again he reached down, put them into the Big Bad Bag and marched back up the mountain towards his cave and the Stinking Stewing Pot.

"Now, here's my dinner for today," he said.

The girls took no notice and played knuckle-bashing in the Big Bad Bag. About halfway to the cave Flat hopped out of the Big Bad Bag and picked off a chunk of sticky resin that was oozing out of a tree trunk.

Again and again she hopped out and ran from tree to tree until she had a great sticky load of it. Then both Flit and Flat smeared it all over the back of Giant Gobbleguts' jacket. When that was done, they hopped out and ran away off home.

Gobbleguts got back to his cave and lay down to rest.

"When I wake up I will have dinner. Oh yes, yes, yes, juicy children for dinner."

He slept and snored for a day or two, but when he tried to get up he found he was stuck to the ground. How he roared and shouted. The mountain shook with the noise of it.

"Waaaaaaaaaaaaaaaaa, I've been tricked!" he wailed.

A few days later Giant Gobbleguts came out of his cave again and marched down the mountain. Flit and Flat came out to meet him and his horrible hairy nose.

"Ah hah! There you are, girls, I was looking for you."

"We were looking for you," said Flit and Flat.

Once again he reached down, put them into the Big Bad Bag and marched up the mountain, back to his cave and the Stinking Stewing Pot.

"Now, here's my dinner for today," he said.

The girls took no notice and played nose-squashing in the Big Bad Bag. About halfway to the cave Flit and Flat hopped out and covered each other with mud. Thick, squelchy mud all over.

Gobbleguts got back to his cave and said, "This time I won't lie down for a rest first. That's how those two little devils tricked me last time. I'll fling them into my Stinking Stewing Pot right now."

And he did, and then lay down to rest.

"When I wake up, I'll have dinner. Oh yes, yes, yes, juicy children for dinner."

He slept and snored for a day or two. Inside the Stinking Stewing Pot the thick mud on Flit and Flat cooled the water down and kept them from burning. When the water was cold enough they sat in the pot scraping the mud off them into the stew. Then they hopped out and ran away off home.

When Giant Gobbleguts woke up he thought, wonderful Children Stew at last. He

got the Stinking Stewing Pot bubbling and boiling and, when it was all hot and steamy, he dipped in his great big spoon and, "YEEEEEEUUUUUUUUUURRRRRRRRRRR RRRRCCCCHHHHHHHHHHHHHHHHHH!!!!! Mud Soup! Waaaaaaaaaaaaa, I've been tricked!" he wailed.

And that was just about as much as he could take of those tricky little twins, and he didn't come down the valley ever again to find children to eat.

The Flat Man

Rose Impey

At night when it is dark
and I am in bed
and I can't get to sleep
I hear noises.

I hear tap, tap, tap.
I know what it is.
It's a tree blowing in the wind.
It taps on the glass.
That's all.

But I like to pretend
it's The Flat Man trying to get in.
His long, bony finger
taps on the glass.
"Let me in," he whispers.
Tap, tap, tap.

I like scaring myself.
It's only a game.

I hear rattle, rattle, rattle.
I know what it is.
A train is going by.
It makes the whole house shake
and the windows rattle,
as if its teeth are chattering.
That's what it is.

But I like to pretend
it's The Flat Man squeezing himself
as thin as he can
through the crack.
"You can't keep me out," he whispers.
Rattle, rattle, rattle.

I hear shsh, shsh, shsh.
I know what it is.
It's my baby brother
making noises in his sleep.
It sounds as if the sea's coming in.

But I like to pretend
it's The Flat Man
sliding around the room.
"I'm coming," he whispers.
Shsh, shsh, shsh.

He keeps his back
close against the wall.
He clings like
a stretched-out skin.
And I know why.

I know The Flat Man's secret.
He's afraid of the light.
He hates open spaces.
That's why he creeps in corners
and drifts in the dark.

One flash of bright light
and he would shrivel up
like a crumpled piece of paper.
The slightest breeze
could blow him away.
So he slips and slides
in the shadows
until he is near my bed.
Then silently
he waits for his chance.

Now I can't hear a sound.
I know what that means.
There is no one there.
No one at all.
But I like to pretend
The Flat Man is holding his breath.
He is waiting
without a sound.
Listen . . .

When everything is quiet
and everything is still,
he will dart over
and slide on to my bed.

I feel a chill down my back.
I know what it is.
There is a little gap
by the skirting board
where the wind blows in.
That's all.

But I pretend
it's The Flat Man
coming closer
and closer,
breathing his icy breath on me.
It makes me shiver.

I pull the covers up
and hold them tight
under my chin.
This is to stop The Flat Man
from creeping into bed with me.

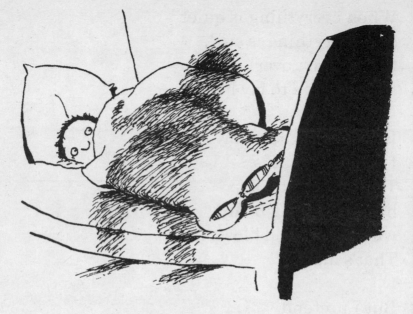

But then I think to myself
he's so thin
he could slide in the smallest crack.
He could creep in
right now . . .
without me knowing.
He could be lying there
already
by my side,
cold and flat.

I lie there afraid to move.
An icy feeling is spreading
all the way up my back.
Someone or something
seems to be wrapping itself
around my chest.

I can't breathe!
I try to think
but my brain is racing round my head.
It won't stop.
There must be something I can do.
Suddenly I remember . . .
The Flat Man's secret!
He doesn't like to be out in the open.
He's afraid he might blow away.

I throw back the covers.
I flap them up and down
like a whirlwind.
"I'll get rid of you," I say.
Flap, flap, flap.

The Flat Man flies in the air.
He is carried
struggling
across the room.
Next I jump out of bed.
I flash my torch at him.
"Take that . . ." I say.
I switch on the lamp.
". . . and that . . ."
I turn on the bedroom light.
". . . and that!"
Flash, flash, flash.

I can hear The Flat Man
cry out in pain.
He starts to shrivel up.
He curls at the edges
and floats towards the window.

I rush to get there first.
I throw it open.
He drifts out on the wind.
He disappears into the black sky.

I close the window
so tight
not even The Flat Man can get in.
SLAM!
"Good riddance," I shout
and I pull a terrible face
just in case
The Flat Man is looking back.

Suddenly my bedroom door opens.
A deep voice says,
"What on earth
do you think you're doing?"

It's my dad.
He looks at me
pulling a face.
"For goodness sake
close those curtains," he says,
"and get into bed."

I creep back.
"I was playing," I say.
"Playing?" says Dad.
"Scaring myself," I say.
"Scaring yourself?" says Dad.

"It's only a game," I say.
"Hmmm," says Dad.
"Well I'll scare you in a minute
and that won't be a game."

He turns off the light.
He shuts the door
and goes downstairs.

Now it is really quiet
and dark again.
I lie in bed.
I screw up my eyes
and I can see shapes.

I can see a big black dragon on the wall.
I know what it is.
It's the kite
my grandad brought me from China.
It hangs from the picture rail.
That's all.

But I like to pretend
it's The Flying Vampire
ready to swoop down on me . . .
Wheeeeee!

Jumo and the Giraffe

Mary Danby

With lazy grace the herd of giraffe wandered among the trees in the clearing, their soft, searching lips moving around the top branches. Then an aeroplane appeared in the sky like a monstrous, noisy bird, and the leader moved off at a spindly canter.

The rest of the herd followed him in a heedless stampede away from the threatening shadow of the aircraft that chased them over the parched ground. Although their movements were casually slow, the giraffe covered so much ground with each stride that they were soon far away from the clump of trees. All except one. Trailing behind the others was a giraffe with an injured leg. Painfully, he limped after them, one sad foot dragging and bumping along the ground.

Jumo was sitting on the branch of a fever tree, watching all this. It was Sunday and he had come out to the bush to be away from the noise and dust of the village, and the chatter of the market and the nagging voice of his mother as she scolded his young brothers and sisters. Here in the wilds, Jumo saw Kenya at its best, the pulsing, relentless sun sending heat shimmers from the yellow grass to the brilliant blue sky.

After the giraffe had gone, a young antelope came and stood only ten feet from where Jumo was sitting. It raised its noble, horned head and sniffed the air. Flies were gathering, and the antelope stamped an irritable foot. Then, with a brisk snort and a shake of its twisted horns, it was off into the trees to join its fellows in the green shade.

An hour passed as Jumo waited, drowsy in the baking heat and thinking how, perhaps next week, he would paint his bicycle in zebra stripes.

A low, purring noise, almost a growl, came

from his left. Jumo sat statue-still as a lioness left the shadows and walked haughtily into the clearing, her golden head held high and proud. She stopped and glanced importantly round, then turned her head to stare at the low bushes behind her. At this signal, a slight movement of leaves and twigs announced the arrival of her two cubs. Like yellow kittens they bounced behind her as she walked on, pretending to stalk her twitching tail.

When this little procession had passed out of sight, Jumo, tired from the effort of keeping so breathlessly still, put his head against the tree trunk and closed his eyes. When he opened them again, the sun had fallen to the treetops, casting evening shadows on the clearing. The giraffe were again among the trees, all facing the setting sun, like a group of toy animals set up by a tidy child.

Jumo started to climb down from the tree. The dusk was no time to be alone in the bush, even if you knew the ways of the wild like your ten times table. He had just reached the foot of the tree when he heard a sound – low, men's voices, quite close to him. Jumo peered round the trunk. Two white men stood talking earnestly. One of them was pointing a stubby, scarred finger towards the giraffe. Both of them carried guns.

Jumo pressed himself against the trunk and thought hard. Here were two hunters, out to kill, not for money – not for fur coats or self-defence – but purely for what they called "sport". If it was sporting to kill a beautiful, harmless creature like the giraffe, then, Jumo decided, he would rather be unsporting.

Suddenly decisive, Jumo ran into the clearing, shouting as loudly as he could and waving his arms in the growing darkness. The giraffe stood perfectly still, listening. Then, with the precision of a well-trained regiment, they turned south and made for cover.

"You! Boy!" shouted one of the hunters. "Stop that noise. You're frightening them away! Stop, do you hear?"

But all Jumo knew was that he must save these animals, *his* animals, from those dreaded rifles. All the giraffe were far away now. Except one. Agonizingly slowly, the lame giraffe hobbled on, its head lifted pathetically high and its eyes desperate and wild.

"Go!" yelled Jumo. "Go! Go! Hurry! Away, away!"

The hunter who had shouted at Jumo caught him on the seat of his trousers with a hefty kick, sending him sprawling. As Jumo lay there, he saw the other man raise his gun and point it at the lame giraffe. With the speed of instinct, Jumo picked up a stone and hurled it at the man. The stone hit the barrel of the gun and it went off with a startling bang.

"Why you— !" The hunter turned his gun on Jumo. "I've had enough of your trouble. There won't be an animal left in the area by now!"

A second bang shattered the air above Jumo. Then another. And another. The first hunter lifted his gun above his head.

"Got him! See? There he goes, the one with the funny leg."

Jumo couldn't look. He knew that the giraffe would be tottering now on feeble legs, like a new-born foal. In a moment it would fall

and its legs would bounce briefly upwards with the impact before lying motionless and stiff on the ground. Perhaps its eyes would still be open.

With a choking cry, Jumo leapt to his feet and ran into the bushes, his sobs echoing through the stillness of the dusk.

A week later, Jumo returned to the clearing. Again he sat in the tree, swinging his legs and thinking about his bicycle. Maybe it would be better to paint it red . . .

A herd of giraffe ambled into the clearing. Jumo wasn't sure whether it was the same herd or not. This time there was no lame member of the group by which to identify it.

When the herd had passed, Jumo came down from the tree and stooped to pick up the empty cartridge cases which still lay where the hunters' guns had dropped them. "Murderers!" thought Jumo, and flung the cartridges hard at the trunk of a tree. He didn't hear the hissing.

Along a branch above his head a huge snake, a deadly python, was waiting – waiting for that finely-timed moment when it could drop on to Jumo's shoulders and wind itself around his thin, brown body, squeezing out life, inch by inch.

One moment Jumo was standing there, scuffing the ground with his canvas shoes, and the next he felt himself gripped by his shirt and hoisted high above the branches. In a flash, as he passed, he saw the menacing snake, then he was carried through the air to the middle of the clearing. Gently, oh so gently, the unseen rescuer returned Jumo to the ground, safely distant from the angry snake.

Jumo looked around, startled and shaken. What could have happened? Who had lifted him so tenderly into the air and saved him from what would surely have been a terrible death?

He gazed around him. There was nothing. Nobody. Or – but it might have been a trick of the light – wasn't there an animal, a tall, ghost-pale animal, moving away among the trees? And there seemed to be something the matter with one of its legs . . .

School Dinners

Jamie Rix

There are some boys and girls who like school dinners. There are others who detest them.

I knew a boy once called Elgin. We used to call him Bluebottle, because he had the manners of a housefly. To say that he liked school food would not do him justice. He worshipped it. He would quite literally fall to his knees at the end of every meal and bow his head in the direction of Matron (any other school would have called her the dinner lady, but my school liked to pretend it was posh, so it *had* to be Matron). For ages I thought he was just being polite, but when I realized that he was in fact licking everyone else's dinner droppings off the floorboards under the table, it made me feel quite sick.

"You are disgusting!" I'd shout.

Elgin's head would appear over the table top, his mouth brimming with pork fat and cauliflower leaves. "Yum, yum," he'd say. "Deeelicious!"

As if this behaviour was not enough to convince me that human beings were still basically animals, who *just happened* to be able to drive cars, Elgin had one further trick up his grubby little sleeve. In the middle of each table was a slop bowl, into which every child would scrape the bits of their meal that they couldn't eat. The fat, the bones, the slugs, the grit and occasionally the potatoes. After he had hoovered up under the table, Elgin would grab the slop bowl, wave it about over his head and enquire if there were any takers. Then, while the rest of us closed our eyes and fought back the rising nausea in our throats, Elgin would down the contents of this bowl in one.

Afterwards he'd always burp, and always say: "Pardon me! Mustn't forget my manners."

I shared a table with Elgin for five years. Little wonder then that over a period of time I slowly came to loathe the sight of school dinners. You cannot imagine how I suffered when Matron slapped a dollop of stewed peas, six pieces of bacon rind and a hunk of liver, still packed full of rubber tubes, on to my plate. She might as well have given me a cowpat to eat. I think I would have preferred it.

My parents got very angry with me. They told me I was stupid and selfish. That there were hungry people who'd give their right arms to eat what I chose to throw away. I would have been happy to send it to them, but Elgin had always eaten my left-overs before I had a chance to wrap them up.

Sometimes, just to please my parents, I would try to look on the bright side.

"What's for pudding?" I'd say cheerfully, as Matron dumped the watery meat stew into my bowl.

"Lumpy, cold rice with sweet cherry jam," she'd reply, "or prunes!"

Was there no escaping this living hell?

The answer, sadly, was no.

I was plagued by Matron. She had got wind of the fact that I did not like my school food and used to shadow me around the dining hall. She lurked behind stacks of freezing cold hotplates, she loitered by the serving hatch, and worst, and most embarrassing of all, she would follow me into the toilet to check that I was not spitting my food out.

"If you don't eat the food, young man," she said to me one day, as I sat staring at a plate of kedgeree, "you will sit here till it gets cold."

"But it's cold already!" I said. "That's why I can't eat it."

Her nostrils flared. "Then you will sit here until it gets even colder or until it's full of maggots, whichever is the sooner!"

"But it's full of maggots already!" I said. "That's why I can't eat it."

Her eye started to twitch. "Then you will sit here until YOU are full of maggots," she said triumphantly.

I didn't want to die in the school dining room.

"Now eat it!" she screamed. A little drop of saliva dripped from the corner of her mouth and settled, like a money spider, on my food. Then she stood over me until I had eaten every last morsel.

This sort of thing went on most days. I got into such a panic about what Matron was going to force me to eat for lunch, that I asked my parents to write me a note, saying that I was the only person in the world suffering from a rare disease called School-dinnerphobia. This was a most unfortunate affliction which meant that if I ate school dinners I would die, instantly, and the person who was in charge of my table would immediately be sent to prison for the rest of her life, for murder. Matron always looked after our table, so I thought that she would probably get the message.

Much to my surprise, my parents sent a note to Matron, along these lines, and it seemed to have the right effect. The day I brought the note in, I was excused from eating school dinner. Matron made me eat the note instead!

I'm sure that had it not been for my unfortunate association with Elgin and Matron I would have had much the same attitude as any other child towards school dinners. As it was, though, I was seriously disturbed. I could not sleep for dreaming of huge rancid chops leaping out from behind doors, pressing me to the ground and demanding to be eaten. The smell of boiled cabbage and burnt custard returned to me with increasing frequency, and then one day, when I was twenty-two years old, I had my first flashback.

I was standing in a tightly packed lift, minding my own business and watching out for my floor, when suddenly my stomach started churning. As I tried to pretend to the onlookers in the lift that it was not *my* stomach making that awful grumbling noise, my mouth joined in. My jaws started to chomp of their own accord. My throat started salivating and the revolting stench of greasy spotted dick filled my nostrils. People were staring at me. I was chewing my tongue like a madman. I tried to smile, but whenever I did I just burped, and every time I burped, a lump of spotted dick popped, from nowhere into my mouth. I couldn't spit it out, not in front of all those people, so, to my complete disgust, I was forced to eat it . . . just as I had been forced to eat spotted dick by Matron, all those years before.

My school dinners had come back to haunt me.

From this day on, things went from bad to worse. The very sight or smell of food would trigger the most alarming responses from within my body. If someone was cooking baked beans I found myself crawling under their kitchen table and shouting: "No! No! NO! I won't come out. I HATE baked beans!"

Carrots had a similar effect *and* tomato ketchup, especially if it reeked of vinegar. I had lost control. Something had taken me over, and I was completely at its mercy.

One night, I took my girlfriend to a very posh restaurant. It was an important evening for me and I was desperate to leave her with the impression that I was a cool, laid-back guy, whom it was well worth getting to know better. The waiter took our coats and showed us to a candlelit table for two in the corner.

"Perfect," I thought, "she's going to love this."

The menu was superb. Lobster, medallions of beef, grilled sole, lamb noisettes and countless other dishes that could not have reminded me *less* of those poisonous school dinners. It was a great relief. I felt confident, for the first time in months, that I was not going to experience a psychic flashback. At the bottom of the menu there was a special notice printed in gold ink. It read:

FOR THE PERFECT NIGHT OUT, WHY NOT TRY OUR CHEF'S SPECIALITY ONLY £125 FOR 2 PERSONS

How could I resist? I ordered champagne, the chef's speciality for two, and sat back to gaze deeply into my loved one's eyes.

A few minutes later, three trumpeters approached our table, stood to attention behind my chair and blew a fanfare. The other people in the restaurant stopped eating and turned to look. The Head Waiter emerged from the kitchens wheeling a trolley, with a huge gold plate on it. The restaurant applauded, my girlfriend laughed, and the Chef's Speciality was ceremoniously brought to our table.

What an evening this was turning out to be.

"With the compliments of the chef," said the Head Waiter, taking the lid off the gold plate.

My stomach lurched, my throat tightened and I could hear Matron chiding me to eat it all up, or else.

"No, I won't!" I shouted, pulling the

tablecloth off the table and upsetting champagne all over my girlfriend. "You can't make
me!"

"Monsieur," said the Head Waiter, who was
a little alarmed. "Is it not to your liking?"

"I HATE FISH CAKES!" I wailed. "THEY
MAKE ME THROW UP!"

Everyone was watching me now, but I
wasn't aware of them. I was back in school.
Even the Head Waiter had started to look like
Matron.

"Eat it up, Monsieur," he said.

"Won't! Won't! Won't! Won't!" I said
clamping my lips tightly shut.

"I shall tell your mummy how naughty you
have been!" said the waiter.

"Don't care! Can't eat fish cakes!" I yelled.
Then I threw a bread roll at him, and
disappeared under the table.

My girlfriend had started crying by now. In
fact she'd left. She had never been so
embarrassed in all her life. I could see her
point.

The Head Waiter was trying Matron's old
trick.

"Shall we park Daddy's car in the garage?" he said holding out a spoonful of fish cake. Then he added, "Brmmm Brmmm! See what a shiny red car it is!"

I poked my head above the table to look, and he grabbed my chin, forcing my mouth open.

"Open the garage doors!" he said loudly. "Because here it comes!"

I yelled and kicked and thumped the table as he tried to force the food into my mouth. I even spat some in his face. In the end, though, I must have eaten the fish cake, because when I woke up on the pavement outside the restaurant it was all round my mouth, like a breadcrumb moustache.

This all happened many years ago. I'm an old man now. Most of my life has been spent in the shadow of this terrible haunting. I still have flashbacks if I see an advert for mashed potato or pass a café selling black chips, but I have found that by living alone and seeing no one, I have been able to keep the ghost of school dinners more or less at bay.

Unfortunately next week is my eighty-third

birthday, and I am going to live in an Old People's Home. I won't pretend I'm happy about it, because I'm not. You see, there's a Matron there (a very familiar-looking Matron), who has promised me that the first thing she's going to do when I arrive is start feeding me up!

Ponkyfoot

David Parker

There was once a terrible pirate called Ponkyfoot. Ponkyfoot was the most dangerous pirate who ever was, and whenever another pirate heard his name his face would turn as white as his toenails and his hands would flutter in the breeze. Ponkyfoot was called Ponky for short.

From a distance Ponky looked a bit like a barrel of tar with a red scarf wound around the top. Just below the scarf, his black eyebrows twitched like crabs' nippers and his black eyes bulged like cannonballs and his angry face was as red as boiling tomatoes.

But the very worst thing about Ponkyfoot was his left leg which was short and thick. It was made from an old ship's timber and it ended in a peg. So that wherever Ponkyfoot walked the leg made a noise so horrible, it would turn your blood to sea water. Ponk! Ponk! Ponk! it went, and everyone else's feet would shake in their boots like jellyfish.

In the harbour below the town lay Ponkyfoot's ship, the bad ship *Thunderbone*.

One night when there was no moon, and the stars were covered with clouds and the water was dark and cold as death, Ponkyfoot decided to put to sea.

"I'll hunt a fine ship and blow her to pieces and leave her sailors in the sea," he thought, "or if there aren't any fine ships to fire at I'll battle with one of me pirate enemies and sink *his* bones to the bottom." And he smiled a horrible smile.

Ponkyfoot looked down fiercely on his scowling pirate crew, standing before him on the fiery deck of *Thunderbone*. There stood Ironhead, his huge hand on a cutlass with a blade as wide as a plank. A scar ran from his nose to his ear and his bald head shone like oil. At the wheel was the grim pirate known as Oyster, saying nothing. He opened his mouth only to eat. Not far from him was a strange figure with a gag in his mouth, jumping up and down. His name was Manywords and he was greatly feared by the other men because he drove them mad with endless talk that no one could understand. Behind the group of frightful men on the deck was perhaps the worst of them all, the great round shape of the evil pirate cook, Glob. These, and the rest of Ponkyfoot's angry crew, stood waiting for their captain's order to sail, as the cold wind cut into their cruel faces.

Ponkyfoot looked over the side, down into the black water flowing past his ship. The tide was beginning to turn. He lifted his head and shouted a command and the strong wind carried his voice like a scrap of paper. The pirates ran over the deck at once. Some of them laid hold of the capstan and others climbed the rigging. Oyster stood ready at the wheel and Glob disappeared below like a squid sliding into a hole. As they worked at their evil ship they sang a terrible song:

Thunder and smoke and blood and bone –
Away, boys, together!
Fear no dead men, cold as stone –
Never, boys, never!

Slowly, the sails filled, and the anchor came dripping out of the sea. Oyster spun the great wheel and *Thunderbone* moved silently out of the harbour and began to rise and fall to the long sea swell. Soon there was no sound on deck but the creaking of spars and ropes and the crash of the sea as the pirate ship lifted and plunged her head like a salty horse. Oyster stood silent as stone at the wheel, gripping its wooden spokes with his thick fingers and looking out into the darkness.

Ponkyfoot paced the deck. Now and then he would clamp his long brass telescope to his eye, looking for signs of a ship he could chase and fight and plunder. But he could see nothing except the grey sea and the white, broken waves. He became angry.

"It's time I found a ship," he growled. "I want gold and dead men's bones." Ponky turned to face his crew. "We want gold, and dead men's bones, don't we lads?" he roared. A fierce shout rose from the men on the deck. Ironhead began to call out a chorus in the howling wind and every pirate on deck lifted his head and joined in the terrible song.

Bones of ships and bones of men shining
in the sun,
Aye! Give us blood and give us gold and
give us Spanish rum!

At that moment, Ponkyfoot heard the sound of a great bell. He saw every one of his pirate crew go stiff with fright. At once the sea was covered with fog. The wind dropped, until there was only the noise of the rocking ship. Then the sound of the bell came again. Every sailor peered out into the fog. Ponkyfoot swung his telescope from one side to another, but he could see nothing, only the swirling mist and the water lying at the sides of the ship. The bell sounded again with a great clang.

"It's the ghost ship," they began to mutter to one another, "the ship no sailor has ever seen and lived to speak of." Whoever saw the ghost ship would join her crew, old sailormen used to say.

Ponky's heart started to bang, his sword shook in his belt and his pipe went out at once. His hands gripped the rails of his ship and his eyes turned towards the place in the fog from which the sound had come. Still he could see nothing. Once again the bell sounded across the water and Ponkyfoot and his pirate crew saw through the cold mist the form of a ship moving silently towards them.

Ponky and his pirates stood quite still on the deck of *Thunderbone*, staring in fear as the ghost ship came nearer. In perfect silence it came closer until it drew alongside *Thunderbone*. At last Ponkyfoot saw its crew.

"They're skeletons!" Ponky whispered. "The bones of dead sailormen!"

White and stiff the sailors of the ghost ship stood upon the deck, and a skeleton held the wheel. Within a moment, the terrible ship sailed by, the mist closed around her, and she was gone.

At that very moment a bell sounded with a loud "Bong!" Ponkyfoot opened his mouth

wide to shout in fear but no sound would come. He gripped the ship's rail and stared out at the grey water. He saw only a great bell rolling in the sea mist, nodding its head like a sleepy old man. A seabird rode on its top, rolling from side to side in the green waves.

"We've seen enough, lads!" Ponky shouted to his pirate crew. "We've seen the ghost ship, that carries off dead sailormen. We'll chase and fight no more. We'll go about and drive for home, lads! Let her run before the wind, away from mist and bones and the ghost ship come to take us."

Soon the shining black ship turned, and began to cut through the sharp, cold waves. Her sails banged and stretched, and *Thunderbone* ran hard towards the sun at the edge of the sea.

But Ponkyfoot and his pirate crew and the bad ship *Thunderbone* were never seen again – not at sea, and not in the harbour. Some people say Ponky has sailed to an island no one has ever seen. But old sailormen talk instead of the ghost ship that carries off dead men. When the sea is wild and the wind is loud and running through the town, *then* you'll hear old Ponky's ghost, they say. When the night is black and full of storm you'll hear his wooden leg. Ponk! Ponk! Ponk! it goes, ringing through the streets. And doors and windows slam and bang and the town goes straight to bed.

Finn's Mistake

Catherine Storr

It was a week before Christmas, and Finn's friends were talking about what they expected to get as presents.

"My dad's going to give me a bicycle," James said.

"My dad's giving me a radio-controlled aeroplane," Nicky said.

"I'm going to get two rabbits, and they're going to have lots and lots of babies," Melanie said.

"Rabbits are stupid. You can't train rabbits to do tricks," Joey said.

"Our dog can go to the shop and bring back the newspaper," Sally said.

"My uncle's got a sheepdog who won in a trial on the telly," said Colin.

Finn had opened his mouth to say that there was a bird in their street which had discovered how to tweak off the foil tops of milk bottles to get at the cream. But now he shut his mouth again. A dog who had won a sheepdog trial was far more exciting than a stealing bird.

"I know someone who keeps a monkey," Joey said.

"I know someone who's got a tame fox," someone else said.

"A real live fox?"

"It lives in a shed at the back, and they give it scraps."

"What are you getting for Christmas?" Nicky asked Finn.

Finn didn't know. His mum had talked about getting him a camera, or a watch. But cameras and watches seemed dull compared to bicycles and monkeys and foxes. He thought of His Animal, which could take any shape he chose, and he said, "I'm going to get a boa constrictor."

No one seemed much interested.

"What's a boa constrictor?" Sally asked.

"A snake. A big huge snake that winds itself round animals and squashes them to death," Finn said.

"Yuk! I wouldn't want a snake like that," Melanie said.

"Where could you keep it?" Nicky asked.

"I don't know. Somewhere."

"Won't your mum mind?" James asked.

"Not as long as I train it so it isn't a nuisance," Finn said.

"Who's going to give you it?" Joey asked.

"My uncle who lives abroad," Finn said.

"I don't believe you. You're making it up," Joey said.

"I'll bring it to school next term. Then you'll see," Finn said. By next term, he reckoned, Joey would have forgotten about the boa constrictor.

Finn forgot about it too. For the next two days he didn't think about anything except Christmas. Helping Mum to make the pudding – "Should have made it months ago, but I expect it'll be all right," she said. Wrapping up his presents for other people, hanging up paper chains and tinsel round the living room, trying to make the fairy lights on the Christmas tree stay lit up. (They wouldn't.) At last, it was time to hang up his stocking before he went to bed. It wasn't really his stocking, it was one of Dad's huge thick walking stockings that came right up to the knee, so that it could hold a lot more than one of Finn's own. Locker had the other one to hang up at the end of his bed.

At last it was quite late on the night before Christmas. Finn was alone in his bedroom and all he had to do was to shut his eyes and go to sleep and then, very soon, it would be Christmas Day.

He went to sleep quite quickly. He dreamed that he was Father Christmas, going the rounds with presents for kids, but nothing went quite right. First of all, the reindeer kept stopping and saying they needed their tanks filled, and Finn didn't know how to satisfy them. Then he worried that he hadn't got enough presents for all the children he should be visiting, and finally, when he had succeeded in persuading the reindeer to land him on a roof, he couldn't get down the chimney, but stuck, with his head and shoulders outside and the rest of him wedged in a chimney. It began to snow. His shoulders were freezing.

He woke up with a start. His duvet had somehow managed to wind itself tightly round his legs and behind and his top half was uncovered and very cold. He turned on his bedside light so that he could re-arrange himself comfortably.

His bedroom looked quite different. The stocking he had hung up was no longer flat and empty. It was bulging and something, he couldn't quite see what, stuck out of its top end. And there were parcels stacked underneath it. A long thin parcel and a knobby, interesting-looking parcel done up with brown paper, a square box-shaped parcel and several small packets with bright paper and ribbons.

It was a rule in Finn's house that you didn't open your Christmas presents until the morning. Open them properly, that is. But if you happened to have torn a corner of the paper, or loosened the string before it was quite daylight, no one was going to take much notice. Finn got out of bed to investigate. First, he shook some of the smaller packets. One of them rattled, but it didn't sound like money, more like marbles. Another smelled deliciously of chocolate. Finn's mouth watered. Two very neatly-packed parcels were certainly books. He turned his attention to the large knobbly parcel; he pushed it a little and found that it was softer in some places, harder in others. It was a most peculiar shape. The brown paper was loose, and Finn managed to prise open a fold so that he could see inside. It was red, his favourite colour, looked like some sort of sack . . . then he realised. It was a backpack, exactly what he'd been wanting. He tidied up the paper so that the place he had peeped through didn't show.

He opened the chocolate-smelling packet and took a bite from a Mars bar. He felt happy. There were still plenty more parcels to open and he enjoyed trying to guess what might be in them.

It was clear that he wasn't going to get all

the things he'd asked for. He had suggested a puppy, but both Mum and Dad had told him straight out that he should give up that idea at once. "If we lived in the country . . ." Mum had said, and Dad had said, "No way am I going to have a dog in this house." A bicycle? Not likely; he'd have to put up with Locker's old machine when Locker had grown out of it, just as he'd had to put up with Locker's old tricycle and sometimes, when they were not too ragged, Locker's second-hand clothes. A radio-controlled aeroplane, like Nicky's? Almost certainly not; he knew that those radio-controlled toys were very expensive. He remembered Melanie and her rabbits; Finn definitely didn't want rabbits for Christmas. Nor did he really want a fox, though he would quite have liked a gorilla.

It was at this moment that he remembered what he had told his friends about his Christmas present. He had said he was going to get a boa constrictor. It had been all very well to say that in the daylight, surrounded by friends, but now, in the night, when he was alone, he should try not to think about a boa constrictor, or any other kind of snake.

But once a thought has come into your head, it is extremely difficult to un-think it. Finn tried. He tried so hard that he stopped eating the Mars bar. But it was no good. He was still thinking, "One of my presents is a boa constrictor."

The large brown paper parcel moved. Finn had propped it up against the bookcase. It now fell over. Finn sat and stared at it. He said to himself, "It just fell over." But he couldn't be sure. And then, just as he had made up his mind that it had been the sort of accident that happens when you haven't propped something up securely, the parcel moved again, this time along the floor towards him.

"No!" Finn cried out, terrified.

The parcel moved a little nearer.

"No! I don't want . . ." Finn began, and then he heard the sound of a door opening and feet coming towards his room. His cry must have woken Mum. In a split second, Finn was back in bed. He had turned off the light, just before his own door was opened and Dad's voice said, "Finn? Anything the matter?"

Finn wished he could snore. He couldn't, so instead, he said, in a sleepy voice, as if he'd just woken up, "Who's that?"

"It's me, Dad. You were calling out, didn't you know?"

"I sort of heard something," Finn said, not wanting to lie too much.

"Must have been dreaming. Go back to sleep, Finn. It isn't time to wake up for Christmas yet." Dad left. As soon as Finn had heard him shut his own door, he turned on his torch and looked at the parcel.

"Are you My Animal?" he asked. He was shaking, but then he'd been out of bed and it was cold.

"Get me out of here," a voice said, muffled by nylon and brown paper. The parcel shook furiously.

"I'll try," Finn said. It was not a task he fancied. Nor was it easy. Although the brown paper had been loosely wrapped round the backpack, it was fastened with far too much sticky tape. That was Dad's doing, he always did up his parcels with this horrible tape which was impossible to peel off, and difficult to cut. What made the job worse was that inside the parcel there was something large and moving, and impatient. Finn was frightened. It might be His Animal, but he'd never seen it as a snake before, and he was sure it was going to be furious with him when at last he got it out.

That did not happen until he had fetched the penknife from his desk, and cut enough of the tape and the paper to free the zip at the top of the backpack. As soon as he'd pulled the zipper back, a head shot out followed by what seemed yards of brown and yellow body, which slithered across the floor and then arranged itself in coils. The head fixed Finn with a beady black eye.

"Don't ever do that to me again," the boa constrictor said.

"Do what?" Finn asked.

"Think of me inside something that I can't get out of. I might have suffocated."

"Sorry! I didn't mean to. It was because I was talking to Nicky about Christmas presents."

"Excuse me. It isn't what you talk about to your friends that decides what I am and where. It's how you think of me when you're alone. You thought of me trapped inside that . . . that thing!" the boa constrictor said.

"That's because I was thinking about how you might be a Christmas present."

"Why should that mean having all that paper and stuff round me?"

"Because people always do wrap up Christmas presents. Like that," Finn said, pointing to the other parcels and packets lying around.

"I wouldn't have been able to get into any of those. Too small. What's inside them?" the boa constrictor asked.

"I'm not sure. Those two must be books. That one had some chocolate." Finn remembered the Mars bar. It was lying half out of its packet. He picked it up and showed it to the boa constrictor.

"You've eaten half of it!" the boa constrictor said.

"Do you want a taste?" Finn held the remains of the bar out towards the boa constrictor's mouth, but the boa constrictor drew back, with an expression of disgust.

"No thank you. Not quite what I am used to. I suppose you haven't got any proper food here?"

"What's proper food?" Finn asked.

"A rat? A mouse, even? I suppose it's too much to ask for a young rabbit?"

"I haven't got anything like that."

"I shall investigate," the boa constrictor said. Finn watched its long mottled body wreathing itself round the packets, sniffing at each one, and leaving it, disappointed. "I wonder if My Animal can be more than one thing at a time? If it could, I could think of it as a rat and then the boa constrictor could eat it. Only it'd be eating itself," Finn thought. It was a muddled thought. He was getting very sleepy.

"Wake up!" the boa constrictor said sharply.

"I'm not asleep."

"You're not far off it. What do you want to do?"

"I'd really like to go back to bed and go to sleep again."

"That's not very adventurous. Think of something more interesting."

"It's the middle of the night," Finn objected.

"We've done things in the middle of the night before now."

"But it's Christmas tomorrow. If I don't go to sleep now, I won't be able to stay awake for it."

If a boa constrictor could shrug its shoulders, this boa constrictor did. Finn felt that it despised him for being so feeble. It said, "Oh, very well. Go back to bed, if that's what you want."

Finn got back into bed. The boa constrictor lay on the floor and looked at him. Somehow Finn didn't much like the way it was looking.

"So what am I supposed to do now?" it asked.

"Couldn't you go to sleep too? After all, it is night."

"I am a nocturnal animal," the boa constrictor said.

"What does that mean?"

"Means I'm awake all night. I sometimes sleep during the day."

"Well, I'm not a noc . . . what you said. I want to go to sleep now," Finn said.

The boa constrictor moved quickly. Finn saw its head appear over the side of the bed and felt its weight coiling across the duvet. "Is it warm in there? I'm cold," it said, wreathing itself round on Finn's chest.

"No!" Finn said, pulling the duvet as tight as he could round his neck to prevent the boa constrictor from getting under it.

"That's not fair! I let you go to sleep, when

I really want to do something exciting, and now you won't even let me in under this cover so that I can warm up. Don't you know that snakes are cold-blooded animals?" the boa constrictor asked.

"I thought that meant you didn't feel the cold."

"It means that I find places where I can get warm. The country I come from is hot. This place is cold. I shall freeze if I have to stay out here all night."

Finn couldn't bear the thought of having a boa constrictor under his duvet. But however much he tried, he couldn't think hard or clearly enough to turn His Animal into anything but the boa constrictor that it was. He was too sleepy and it was so very large and heavy, so very brown and yellow, so very near. He said, "Look! I'll find something to keep you warm, I promise. Only not my duvet. I wouldn't be able to sleep at all if you were under here with me."

"Where, then?" the boa constrictor asked.

Finn shone his torch round his room. There was coloured paper, the end of a Mars bar, the

90

half-unwrapped backpack on the floor. He saw his clothes on the chair. "You could wrap yourself in my pullover?" he suggested.

The boa constrictor slid off the bed and investigated the chair. If Finn hadn't been so sleepy and frightened he'd have laughed to see the creature trying to get into his pullover. It got its head into a sleeve and stuck there. When it had jerked itself free, it put its head out of the neck opening and its tail appeared at the end of the other sleeve. But it was clear that the pullover wasn't nearly big enough. It wouldn't cover even half of the great snake's body.

"What's that?" it asked suddenly, pointing with its nose.

"That's my Christmas stocking."

"What's it got in it? Anything for me to eat?" But before Finn could answer that question, the boa constrictor had slithered across and caught the stocking in its mouth and had pulled it down to the floor. Finn saw it rapidly tip out the contents on to the floor. Finally, after a good deal of writhing and what sounded like cursing, it managed to cover itself almost completely underneath Finn's pullover and the stocking.

"That's better," Finn heard it say.

"But you've spilled all my stocking presents! and you've bitten a hole in Dad's stocking toe!"

"Of course if you'd rather I came into bed with you . . .?" the boa constrictor said, sticking its head out from under the woolly mountain.

"No!"

"Very well, then. Now, keep quiet."

"I'm going to sleep now," Finn said. He hoped the boa constrictor would stay where it was. He didn't fancy it back on his bed, trying to find a way to get under the duvet.

He switched off the torch. Nothing moved in the darkness. Finn slept.

"Wake up!"

"Wake up!" It was Locker's voice.

"Wha . . . at? What's the matter?" said Finn, still asleep.

"It's Christmas! It's morning. Well, almost." Locker turned on the light.

"What happened? You've taken everything out of your stocking! You've made a horrible mess," he said, and Finn had to agree. On the floor by his bed lay his pullover, his Christmas stocking, and various small objects which it had contained, as well as torn paper, a tangerine, shreds of ribbon and coloured paper. The boa constrictor had not been idle during the night.

"Mum won't be pleased," Locker said.

"I didn't mean . . ." Finn began.

"You'd better clear up that mess before she comes in. I'll help," Locker said, full of Christmas kindness. Finn saw him put out a hand towards the stocking. "Take care!" he'd cried out before he knew he was going to say anything.

"Take care of what? It's not going to bite," Locker said.

Finn thought of saying, "No, but it might wind itself round you and crush you to death." But as he looked, Locker picked up the stocking, which hung, flat and empty from his hand.

"You're still dreaming," Locker said, busily

putting the stocking-fillers back where they belonged.

"I'm all right. Thanks, Locker. Have you opened your stocking yet?"

"Brought it in here so we can open them together, like always. I ate my Mars bar. Did you?"

"I ate some of it." Finn looked around. "It doesn't seem to be here," he said.

"I expect you ate the rest of it in your dream. Here's your stocking. Now, let's open them at the same time. One, two, three, Go!"

But though Finn later searched very carefully all over his now tidy bedroom floor, he never found the second half of the Mars bar.

Teeny-Tiny and the Witch-Woman

Barbara K. Walker

Once there was and twice there wasn't, long ago, a family with three brothers – Big-One, In-the-Middle, and Teeny-Tiny. Every day their mother said, "You can play anywhere in the village, but do not go into the forest to play. Your granny says a witch-woman lives there, where the trees are darkest. She eats little children, and uses their bones to make the fence around her house."

Big-One and In-the-Middle laughed, but Teeny-Tiny shivered. He was glad to play there in the warm sunshine, away from the forest.

One morning, though, when no one was looking, Big-One said, "Let's go into the forest to play."

"Yes," agreed In-the-Middle. "I'm not afraid of any old witch-woman! Come on, Teeny-Tiny."

Now Teeny-Tiny didn't want to go, but he went anyway. "I'll keep my eyes open and my legs ready to run," he told himself.

Big-One, In-the-Middle, and Teeny-Tiny played all day in the forest. The deep, dark shadows made fine hiding places, and the wild berries in the clearings made a delicious lunch.

Little by little, the shadows grew longer. The boys looked for the path to the village, but no matter where they looked they could find no path at all. At last Teeny-Tiny climbed a tree to look farther. "I see a light," he called. "Let's go there. It may be a house."

They walked and they walked till they came to a little house, all by itself in the darkest part of the forest. All around the house there was a knobbly white fence. The gate clattered as they pushed at it.

Just then, the door of the house opened, C-R-E-A-K, and an old woman stood in the doorway. But what a strange old woman she was, with her nose turned down and her chin turned up, and just the points of her teeth showing.

"Come in. Come in, my children!" she called. And she beckoned with her bony finger.

Big-One and In-the-Middle started towards the open door, but Teeny-Tiny whispered, "Wait! Remember what our granny said."

"Oh, that can't be the witch-woman," said Big-One. "She's so kind to ask us in."

"I'm tired," said In-theMiddle. "You're just *afraid* because you're *little*."

"Afraid?" The old woman cackled. She had heard them! "You needn't be afraid of *me*. I *love* little children. Come in," she coaxed. "Stay with me and share my dinner. Your own nice, warm beds are far away, but I have room for all of you in my little house tonight. Tomorrow I shall show you your way home. But come now, and smell the good dinner I have ready for you."

And the old woman hobbled over to the fireplace. She took off the lid of her huge iron kettle, and, *Mmmmn*, what good smells came out of that kettle!

"Come on," said Big-One. "I'm going inside."

"Good boy," said the old woman. "You may call me Auntie." And she waited by the door as In-the-Middle and Teeny-Tiny followed Big-One into the house.

While the old woman set three extra places at the dinner table, Teeny-Tiny looked around at all that he could see. Over in the corner of the room was a crooked little wooden cage. "Auntie," he asked, "what do you keep in your cage?"

"In my *cage?* Oh, sometimes I keep stray dogs and sometimes I keep stray cats," answered the old woman.

"And sometimes stray *children*?" wondered Teeny-Tiny. But he didn't say anything.

It was a very good dinner that the old woman scooped up out of the kettle, with bits of tender meat and plenty of rice. The boys ate and ate, and the good food and the warm fire made them very sleepy.

"You must be tired," said the old woman. "Come now, into the bedroom and I'll put you into my nice, soft beds." Sure enough, she tucked Big-One into one bed, In-the-Middle into a second bed, and Teeny-Tiny into a third bed. "Now sleep well," she said, "and tomorrow, just *see* if I don't show you your way home!" Leaving the door ajar, she went out into the kitchen.

Teeny-Tiny waited until he heard her picking up the dishes, and then he tiptoed to the window to look outside. The moon had risen, and the moonlight shone down on that knobby white fence. Was it a *wooden* fence? No. It was made of *bones* – leg bones and arm bones, little *people* bones. Teeny-Tiny stared at the fence, and then he looked at Big-One and at In-the-Middle, already sound asleep. They didn't know, but Teeny-Tiny did.

This was indeed the house of the witch-woman their granny had told them about!

Teeny-Tiny tiptoed back to bed. As he lay there, he could see the old woman tying pieces of rope together. He could hear her sharpening and sharpening a great, long knife. And all the while she hummed a sleep-sleep-sleepy song.

After a while, the old woman called, "Who is awake and who is asleep?"

Now the others were asleep, but Teeny-Tiny was not.

"The littlest one is awake," he answered.

"What! Teeny-Tiny, why don't you sleep?" asked the old woman.

"Well, Auntie, my mother always cooks me an egg before I go to bed. *Then* I go to sleep," said Teeny-Tiny.

So the old woman cooked an egg, and Teeny-Tiny ate it. But still he did not go to sleep.

After a while she called again, "Who is awake and who is asleep?"

"The littlest one is awake," answered Teeny-Tiny.

"What? Still awake? What will help you to sleep?" the old woman asked.

"Well, Auntie, my mother gives me popcorn and raisins to eat at bedtime. *Then* I go to sleep," said Teeny-Tiny.

So the old woman brought him popcorn and raisins. But still he did not go to sleep.

After a while she called again, "Who is awake, and who is asleep?"

"The littlest one is awake," answered Teeny-Tiny.

"What! Still awake, are you? What can I get you that will help you to sleep?" she asked.

"Well, Auntie, all that popcorn has made me thirsty. At home, when I am thirsty, my mother goes to the well to fetch me water in a sieve. When she brings it back, I drink it. *Then* I go to sleep," said Teeny-Tiny.

As the old woman bent over to fetch her sieve, a cake of soap fell out of her apron pocket. "Oh dear," the old woman mumbled aloud. "My magic objects. Better to leave them here safe than lose them outside in the dark by the well." She picked up the cake of soap. Then, reaching into her apron pocket, she took out what was left – a needle and a short, sharp knife – and she laid all three things on a high shelf. Then she opened the door softly and started towards the well.

All along, Teeny-Tiny had been listening carefully. As soon as the old woman was gone, he shook his brothers. "Wake up!" he whispered. "Auntie *is* that witch-woman! Her fence is made of people's bones, and she has already sharpened her long knife. If we do not hurry, *we'll* be her dinner tomorrow." Big-one and In-the-Middle heard him, and how they scrambled out of bed!

As they were running through the door, Teeny-Tiny remembered the magic objects the witch-woman had so carefully laid on the high shelf – a cake of soap, a needle, and a short, sharp knife.

"Lift me up," he said to Big-One. "If she *says* they're magic, they just may *be* magic. I'll take them along and see." One, two, three – he tucked them into his pocket, and then ran with his brothers down the moonlit path.

As for the old woman, she couldn't catch any water in the sieve, and she *couldn't* catch any water in the sieve. And because witches are not very bright without their magic, she couldn't understand why. So home she went.

When she looked for Teeny-Tiny he was gone, and so were his brothers. So away she went, running after them.

Now, Teeny-Tiny was watching behind him. As the old woman came closer and closer, he took out the cake of soap. "I'll try this first," he said. "If it *isn't* magic, at least she may slip on it, and then we can get away from her."

And he threw the cake of soap right into her path.

"Oh!" she cried. "You took my magic soap from my little shelf!" And she shook her fist at Teeny-Tiny. Just then, the cake of soap began to *grow* and GROW. It became a

mountain, slippery all around. The boys kept on running, glad of that soap.

But the old woman slipped and slithered, trying to get up over the mountain. "It's no use," she said at last. "I'll run around it." And she ran and ran till she came to the other side. "Now I'll catch you!" she cried. And Teeny-Tiny heard her.

They kept running and running, till Teeny-Tiny could hear the witch-woman's apron flapping.

Then carefully, he picked the needle out of his pocket. "Whether it's magic or not, I'll prick her with this sharp needle," he said to himself. But, *whoops!* It slipped out of his hand and fell behind him.

"Oh!" cried the witch-woman. "You found my magic *needle,* too!" And she shook her fist at Teeny-Tiny. At that moment, the needle began to *grow* and GROW, until it became a whole mountain of needles, all sticky and pricky and sharp as they could be.

Well, the boys ran on, but the witch-woman had to stop because of the needles. She tried and tried to get over those needles. At last she said, "It's no use. I'll run around them." And she ran and ran till she came to the other side. "*Now,* I'll catch you!" she cried.

They kept running and running and running. Teeny-Tiny could hear the old woman panting and puffing just behind them. With all his strength, he threw the knife on the path right in front of the witch-woman. "It's our only chance," he said. "If it *isn't* magic, at least she may cut her foot on it, and then we can get away from her."

"Oh!" she cried. "You took my magic *knife,* too!" And she shook her fist at Teeny-Tiny. At that moment, CRICK-CRACK! That sharp knife cut a crack in the earth so long and so wide that the witch-woman couldn't run around it, and she couldn't jump over it. Shaking both fists, she shouted, "I'll get you the *next* time!" And she turned around and hobbled home.

The three boys never stopped running till they got to their own house. As for that witch-woman, may she wait a long, long time before she hears a knock at her door again.

Cherry-Berry

Michael Rosen

Cherry-Berry lived with her dad. Her mum had died some time before and ever since then things hadn't gone very well. Dad had changed. He'd become sad and hopeless and didn't look after her properly. He went out at night, leaving her all alone in the house. Cherry-Berry missed her mum and wanted her to come alive again. She kept a picture of her by the side of her bed, and she always remembered something that her mother had told her: One is weak, many are strong. She wasn't sure she knew what it meant but she liked the sound of it.

One night, her dad was out playing cards with his friends in a little house at the edge of town. This night, like most nights, he was losing. Try as he might, he couldn't win and he was losing money again and again. He kept saying to himself, "If I could win just once, I'd go home. If only I could win just once – that's all I ask."

Then, faster than it takes to swallow a baked bean, a little knobbly man put his head round the corner and said to Cherry-Berry's dad, "You can win all the money you want if you do something for me."

"And what is it I'd have to do for you?"

"You must give me the first thing you speak of when you get home," said the little knobbly man.

"Well, that's easily done," said Cherry-Berry's dad. He thought how he could walk in at home and say, "I fancy a nice fresh slice of bread," or "Are we short of carrots?" and then he could give the little knobbly man a slice of bread or some carrots.

"Yes," said Cherry-Berry's dad, "that's easily done."

"Do you promise on the stars?" said the little knobbly man.

"I promise," said Cherry-Berry's dad. "Now

let's get on with the game. I want to win."

So, Cherry-Berry's dad sat down at the table and, sure enough, he won. And he went on winning till the others wouldn't play any more. Now he had more money in his hand than he had seen in years and he went home a happy man.

"Cherry-Berry!" her dad called out. "We have money, my girl, no more worries."

The moment he said it, he clapped his hand over his mouth, but it was too late to stop the word coming out. He'd said it now.

"What's the matter?" asked Cherry-Berry. She was well used to his strange and reckless ways. "Is something wrong?"

"Yes," said her dad. "I've done something terrible. A little knobbly man said he could help me win at cards if I gave him the first thing I spoke of when I got home. And the first thing I said was your name, Cherry-Berry."

"I'll have to think of something," said Cherry-Berry, and she took herself to bed.

In the morning Cherry-Berry said to her father, "Tell the little knobbly man that the

first thing you spoke of was Cherry-Berry –
it's a girl, and she'll be coming in a red dress."

So off went Cherry-Berry's dad to the little
house at the edge of town, and he called out,
"Little man, little man, where are you?"

And a voice came from the house, "I'm here,
what will you bring me?"

"Cherry-Berry," said Cherry-Berry's dad.

"And how will I know this Cherry-Berry?"

"She's a girl and she'll be wearing a red
dress."

Meanwhile, Cherry-Berry went off to
school to find her friends.

"Listen," she said, "you've got to help me.
When the morning school's over, run home,
change into red dresses and come with me to
the edge of town."

And that's what they did.

Just before twelve o'clock a long line of
girls in red dresses made their way to the
house at the edge of town. Suddenly the little
knobbly man appeared and said, "Where is
Cherry-Berry?"

"I am Cherry-Berry," said the first girl.

"I am Cherry-Berry," said the second girl.

"I am Cherry-Berry," said the third girl. And so on through all the girls.

"BAH!" shouted the little knobbly man. He rushed away shouting, "You won't get away with this, you won't get away with this."

Cherry-Berry went home and when her dad got in later he was delighted to see her.

"Listen, Dad," said Cherry-Berry, "you may see the little knobbly man again. If you do, tell him I will come and I'll be wearing a white dress."

"Oh no," said her dad. "I'm not going back there again. I'm staying here to look after you."

But that night, after Cherry-Berry had gone to bed, once again he went off to play cards with his friends in the little house at the edge of town. But no sooner had he sat down at the table to play than out popped the little knobbly man.

"Why did you play that trick on me?" he shouted.

"I did just as you told me to," said Cherry-Berry's dad.

"Make sure she comes tomorrow," said the

little knobbly man. "How will I know it's her?"

"She'll be wearing a white dress," said Cherry-Berry's dad.

"And she'd better be, or you will be struck down dead."

In the morning Cherry-Berry's dad had to tell her what had happened.

So later, Cherry-Berry and her friends made their way to the edge of town dressed in white.

Out came the little knobbly man again. "Who is Cherry-Berry?"

"I am Cherry-Berry," said the first girl.

"I am Cherry-Berry," said the second girl.

"I am Cherry-Berry," said the third girl. And so on through all the girls.

The little knobbly man roared with anger. "You won't get away with this," he said, "you won't get away with this!" and disappeared.

Cherry-Berry went home and when her dad got in he was delighted to see her.

"Listen, Dad," said Cherry-Berry, "you may see the little knobbly man again. If you do, tell him I'll be wearing a black dress."

"Oh no," said her dad. "I'm not going back

there again. I'm staying here to look after you."

But that night, after Cherry-Berry had gone to bed, once again he went off to play cards with his friends in the little house at the edge of town. No sooner had he sat down at the table to play than out popped the little knobbly man.

"Why did you play that trick on me?" he shouted.

"I did just as you told me to," said Cherry-Berry's dad.

"Make sure she comes tomorrow," said the little knobbly man. "How will I know it's her?"

"She'll be wearing a black dress," said Cherry-Berry's dad.

"And she'd better be, or your house will fall down with you in it."

In the morning, Cherry-Berry's dad had to tell Cherry-Berry what had happened.

But this time Cherry-Berry and her friends didn't go to the house at the edge of town. The little knobbly man waited and waited for her there, and when she didn't come he rushed down the road with a face like thunder.

"They won't get away with this," he shrieked. And when he got to Cherry-Berry's house he shouted, "Come out, come out, I want what was promised me."

But there was no answer.

"Right, I'm coming in!"

And in he rushed.

But Cherry-Berry and her friends had opened the door in the floor that led down to the cellar. In rushed the little knobbly man and down he fell into the cellar and Cherry-Berry slammed the door shut after him. The little knobbly man was locked tight in the cellar.

"Let me out! Let me out!" shouted the little knobbly man.

"Oh no," said Cherry-Berry. "Not you nor anyone like you."

When her dad came home later, he was delighted to see her.

"I didn't go to the little knobbly man this time, Dad," she said.

"And what happened?"

"He came here. He was angry because he

couldn't have what you promised him."

"So then what happened?"

"Well, I was angry because you promised him something you should never have promised."

"So?"

"He's in the cellar."

"How did he get there?"

"We put him there."

So Cherry-Berry and her dad collected up all their things and ran out of the house. The last thing they heard was the little knobbly man shouting, "Right, your house will fall down with you in it!"

There was a crack, and a rumble, and a roar, and the house fell down and no one ever saw the little knobbly man again.

"Now we can go somewhere else to live," said Cherry-Berry, "and start a new life there."

"You're right," said her father, and he promised he'd never go back to the little house at the edge of the town again. And he didn't.

Cherry-Berry and her father lived together

happily in their new home, and Cherry-Berry would often look at the picture of her mother by the side of her bed and think of her mother's old saying: One is weak, many are strong.

The Haunted Cave

Sydney J. Bounds

"And what's Minnehaha feel like doing today?"

Minnie Jackson stuck out her tongue. The boys knew she hated being called Minnehaha, and never tired of teasing her about being part-Indian. She ran ahead, between spruce and evergreen, so they wouldn't see her face. She didn't want them to see how close she was to tears. Sometimes she wished she wasn't part-Indian.

Minnie, Ed and Dan Laine, with their parents, were on a camping holiday in the Rocky Mountains. Both Ed and Dan were older than Minnie, and insisted on treating her like a little girl, even though she wore jeans and a check shirt just like theirs.

Further up the hill track, beyond the pines, Bandy – Ed's dog – began to bark excitedly.

"A cave up there," Dan said, shading his eyes against bright sunlight. "Let's explore."

Ed looked doubtful. "Pretty steep climb – our squaw'll never make it."

Nine-year-old Minnie, furious, snapped, "I will, I will too," and scrambled up the rock and dirt slope ahead of them. She was panting when she reached the ledge in front of the cave, high above their lake-side camp. Only Bandy was before her.

Dan and Ed arrived, looked at the dark hole in the hillside; the top of the hill was a good bit higher. "Looks like rain washed some rockfall away," Dan said. "This opening's a new one."

They peered inside, curious about what they might find there. Cloud passed across the sun and the air turned suddenly chill. Minnie shivered.

In the cave mouth, a shadow-shape seemed to form in the air, something big and shaggy. Minnie looked, and in that moment, it vanished.

Ed was startled. "For a moment, I thought I saw a grizzly – couldn't have been, none in this area for a long time."

"Nothing there now," Dan said, but the boys advanced with less enthusiasm.

They paused in the opening, half in the sunlight, half in the shadow; the cave looked uninviting. An animal sound came from deep inside, a throaty roar, like a challenge.

Bandy, ears down and tail between hind-legs, scooted down the hill.

Ed frowned. "Bandy never acted that way before – he's not usually scared of anything."

"Must be some wild animal's den. Better get back down, I guess."

The sound changed to a low cry, like the squalling of a baby, and Minnie stopped and looked back.

"That's an animal in pain," she said. "It's hurt and needs help – I'm going in."

"Don't be a nut, Minnie – an injured animal can turn savage!"

Minnie ignored this remark. She liked animals and found they trusted her. She stepped boldly into the dark cave.

"Come back," Dan called.

She walked further inside. Beyond the entrance, the cave widened. High up, through a gap in the roof, sunbeams slanted down, lighting the bare rock. She saw only fallen boulders and moss, nothing living – though there had been at one time. There was a scattered heap of bones.

A stillness hung in the air, as if the cave waited for something . . .

"It's all right," she called back, her voice echoing. "There's nothing here – the place is empty."

Dan and Ed came warily into the cave and looked around.

Then the challenging roar sounded again. Ed started, "Just the wind in the cracks, I guess," he said uneasily.

A shadow-shape formed in the air before them, huge, monstrous. Revealed in the sunbeams, surrounded by the dark walls of the cave, it appeared much more lifelike than before.

It lumbered on legs thick as tree trunks, covered in matted hair; the ears were rounded and the black rubbery nose wrinkled. There was a strong animal smell. Red eyes glinted at them.

"Grizzly – run for it!"

Scared, the two boys bolted from the cave.

Minnie stayed behind, alone. Her legs felt numb and she was unable to move. She wasn't frightened, not really; this was more like a dream she was having. She stared, fascinated at the bear-shape until it faded away before her eyes.

The squalling sound started again, and she felt a surge of pity. "There must be a small animal trapped in here," she thought; she had to find it and help it.

Her legs were all right now and she began to search the cave, calling, "Where are you? You poor thing, I only want to help."

She went all round the cave again, looking behind boulders, inside cracks in the walls, but she found nothing. She stood in the sunbeams, puzzled, looking round, thinking hard – and her gaze settled on the bones.

She looked closer and saw that there were two separate piles, one big and twisted, and a smaller heap a little way away. She studied them a moment and looked up at the roof, at the gap where the sun had shone.

It was obvious, really, she told herself, the bear cub had fallen down and the big she-bear had tried to climb down to rescue the cub – and fallen, breaking a leg. There hadn't been this lower opening to the cave then, and so they were trapped.

Minnie felt very sad as she imagined it all, the injured she-bear and her young cub, starving. She shivered. No wonder their spirits never got out of the cave . . . she was thinking like an Indian now, she realized, and memory of one of Gran's tales came back to her. Gran had much more Indian blood in her veins, of course, and Minnie had listened fascinated to her stories.

"Before my time, Indians had to kill bears for food, but they didn't like doing it. Afterwards, great care was taken to lay out the bones properly, so the bear would not be crippled in the spirit world."

Now Minie knew what she had to do.

Very carefully, she began to move the

bones, setting the broken leg straight to enable the she-bear to walk again. Then she moved the bones of the cub next to her mother.

She stood back, watching – and seemed to see two shapes form in the sunbeams, one huge and shaggy, the other small, scampering along at the she-bear's side. Together they went out through the new opening in the hillside.

Minnie went after them, blinking in the strong sun – and they vanished.

The cave was silent now, and Minnie felt happy she had been able to help – and suddenly proud she was part-Indian. She would never mind again if the boys called her Minnehaha.

She stopped once to look back before going down the hill to the campsite and her parents. Both piles of bones had turned to dust. A fresh breeze blew gently through the cave, scattering the dust till nothing was left.

The Sorcerer's Apprentice

Retold by Felicity Trotman

High in the mountains in a remote part of Germany, there was an old castle. It clung to the crags as though it was afraid of falling into the deep ravine that fell away from it on one side, while on the other side great dark trees grew up to the walls, and whispered secret things when the winds blew.

Only two people lived in the castle, a man and a boy. The man was a sorcerer, wise and ancient. The boy was his apprentice.

The sorcerer spent most of his time in the great hall of the castle. Here were benches crowded with strange vessels, crucibles, torts, limbecs, and the like, along with silver basins; great bunches of magical herbs – moly, foxgloves, hypericum and artemesia.

There were piles of books, too. Some were so precious they were chained to the wall, and many were written in old, forgotten languages. On one wall hung a great mirror that did not reflect, in the window stood an orrery and an astrolabe, and a crocodile lived in the vault of the roof.

The boy spent most of his time in the castle kitchen. He had to clear up after his master, and look after him as a servant would have done. But he knew that he too had magic powers – was that not why the sorcerer had chosen him as an apprentice in the first place? He longed to try them out, but his master would not let him practise anything but the most minor spells and lesser magics.

"It will be many years," the magician often said to him, "longer than most men's lives, before you have learned enough to begin to call yourself a magician."

The boy was forbidden to enter the great

hall when his master was working great magic. Sometimes, though, he disobeyed and peeped round a crack in the door.

He had seen marvellous things – piles of pebbles changed to shining gold, dragons and princes summoned up at a word, and the magician watching both past and future in the dark mirror.

He tried to remember everything he had ever heard his master say and seen his master do, and burned with a fierce longing to try out these wonders for himself.

Day after day, though, the same life went on. Always the sorcerer stayed in his hall, and the boy fumed in the kitchen.

Then, one night, the sorcerer summoned his apprentice. "Tonight I am going to watch the stars," he said. "There is a rare conjunction of planets, and the wise may learn much of the future by observing it. While I am gone, fill up the largest cauldron. I shall need plenty of hot water as soon as I return."

Now the river that supplied the castle was some distance away, and the poor boy groaned when he heard the magician's words. He had worked hard all day, and must now work hard for a good part of the night also. It would take many journeys down to the river to fill the enormous cauldron that was hardly ever used, and he did not look forward to trudging uphill with so many heavy buckets of water.

First of all, he built up the kitchen fire, making sure that there was a good supply of logs beside it. Then he swung the jack out and, with great effort, hooked the huge cauldron onto it. He picked up the yoke, and put a bucket on the end of each chain.

Then he had a brilliant idea. "For once in a blue moon, the old witch-master has gone out," he said to himself. "Now's my chance! I've been longing to try out a spell or two on my own. At last I can use my magical powers and do myself a favour as well. I've watched the old man so often, I know exactly what to do."

He crept quietly out of the kitchen, half-afraid that his master would come in and find him.

In the first great hall, he found a small ebony wand which belonged to the sorcerer.

His hand tingled as he picked it up. When he was back in the kitchen, the apprentice went into the corner where the mops and brooms were kept. He picked up the oldest broomstick, which he usually used for sweeping leaves up in the yard, and he propped it against a chair.

"Listen, old broomstick," he said. "You've worked round here for a long time. Now you are going to take orders from me. Stand up on your own two legs! We'll have a head on top of you so that you can see where you're going, too. Now, pick up the buckets, and hurry up and fill that cauldron!"

Deeply excited, he clutched the wand firmly. He made some mystical movements in the air, and repeated the words of the spell that would complete his magic:

"Old broom, old broom, get up and go,
To the river make your way.
The cauldron fill,
(For that's my will)
You will make the water flow,
Until the magic word I say."

To his great delight, the old broom came to life at once. The apprentice watched gleefully as it sprang up the steps to the kitchen door. He ran up the steps after it, hardly believing what he saw as he watched it hurry down the path to the bank of the river, fill up the buckets, and come running back up the hill. The boy stood aside as the broom crossed the threshold, made its way down the steps and poured the water into the cauldron.

"Just look at it," he murmured. "It's working so fast that the cauldron will be filled in no time."

For some time the boy went on watching the hard-working broomstick. How good it was to sit by the fire, and not to have to toil up the path in the dark with those heavy buckets! He was very pleased with the success of his spell.

"That'll show the old man," he thought. "Maybe now I can convince him that I'm ready to move onto bigger things. No more messing around with the washing-up for me!"

By this time the cauldron had filled up nicely. As the broomstick came in with the

next load of water, the apprentice stood up. He thought he'd got enough in the cauldron for the magician's purposes, so he picked up the wand once more and pointed it at the broomstick, trying to put an end to the spell.

"Stand still, stand still!
The cauldron's full . . ."

he began, and then his voice sank to a whisper as he realized what had happened. "What shall I do? I've forgotten the words of the spell to make it stop!"

Desperately the boy tried to remember what he had seen the sorcerer do. He tried every word and every magic pass he had ever seen him make, but it was no good. None of them worked on the broomstick.

All this time the broomstick was bringing in buckets of water. The cauldron was overflowing onto the floor long before the apprentice stopped his attempts at magic-making. Wishing with all his might that he had the plain old broomstick back again, he grabbed the handle as the stick went past him with yet more buckets of water. The head he had conjured up turned and glared at him so angrily that the boy let go, and took a step backwards. He felt very frightened. Then he noticed that water was creeping under the door which led out into the great hall. Cautiously he opened it. By the light of the single torch that lit the great room, he saw to his horror that the water was running in a steady stream into the hall.

"Just look at that water," he moaned. "If it gets into the hall and damages my master's belongings, I'll be lucky if he only throws me out for ever. Oh, you cursed broom, why won't you listen to me?

"Broom, stand still!"

But the broom paid no attention. It carried on pouring water out of the buckets into the overflowing cauldron.

The apprentice thought long and hard. There must be *something* he could do to stop the thing! He stared round the kitchen. Then his eye fell on the hatchet he used to cut firewood. "Aha!" he thought. "The very thing.

I'll chop the broomstick up. That'll stop it."
He waded across the floor, picked up the
hatchet, and grasped the haft very firmly.

When the broom returned from its next trip
to the river, the apprentice seized it. It
struggled furiously, and he had to fight hard
before he was able to pin it flat over the seat of
a chair, holding it down with one foot. But the
hatchet was sharp, so it did not take him long
to chop the stick into two.

"Hurrah," he said to himself, as the two
pieces splashed into the water. "That's done
it. Now I can breathe freely again."

But to his horror, the two pieces rose
dripping from the floor. Now they *both* had
legs and heads!

The new broom collected a yoke and
another pair of buckets, and both of them
went up the kitchen stairs, out of the door,
and down the path to the river. Still working
at great speed, both brooms continued to
bring back water, wading through the rising
tide in the kitchen to pour it into the
cauldron – just as they had been instructed to
do. But now the water rose twice as fast as

before. The fire had long ago been put out by all the water.

The apprentice was terrified. "I'm going to drown," he said, and he clung to the table, which was now floating round the kitchen, in an effort to save himself. Sobbing with fright as he felt it bumping into the pots and logs which were also floating, he thought at last of the one thing that might save him. "Help!" he shouted, as loudly as he could. "Help! Master, come and rescue me!"

And to his great relief, there stood the sorcerer, outlined in the doorway and looking grimly down at the watery mess.

"Please sir," the apprentice gasped, "I'm in terrible trouble. I put a spell on the broomstick to make it do the work you set me, and I can't stop it." He did not care any longer about the trouble he was in. Anything would be better than all this water!

The sorcerer looked at the twin broomsticks as they came past him with four more buckets of water. He leaned down into the flood, and picked up the ebony wand as it came sailing past him. Shaking the water off it, he held it up, and the wind blowing through the open door made his long cloak swirl about him. He moved his hand once, in a great circle, and said,

"Enough, enough, old broom, old broom,
Back to the corner of the room."

The apprentice watched in wonder as the two parts of the broomstick merged together. With a rattle, one broomstick propped itself up in the old corner – and the flood vanished, leaving the big cauldron full of hot water, a brightly burning fire, and the kitchen just as dry as it usually was. Thankfully, he got down off the table.

"Come with me," the sorcerer said. He picked up the broomstick, and strode off into his hall. The apprentice was thankful to see that here too the floor was dry and everything looked as usual. Without even taking off his cloak, the magician placed the broomstick in the centre of the pentagram, the magic star painted on the floor. This was where the most powerful spells were worked, and the apprentice quailed, though he was so fascinated he could not stop watching.

"Remember, broomstick!" said the sorcerer. "From now on, the only person who will ever be able to put a spell on you is I, your master." And having sent the broomstick back to the kitchen under this strong protection, he turned to his apprentice, who was shaking with fright. "As for you—" the sorcerer said fiercely –

"Please sir," gasped the boy, "please sir, I'm sorry. I'm dreadfully sorry. I promise I won't do it again – but please don't stop me learning magic. I couldn't bear that."

His master looked startled. "Indeed?" He paused. "It's true that I would have to search hard before I found a lad with as much natural ability as you have. Maybe I have been at fault in instructing you too slowly. I judge that the lesson you have learned tonight will teach you more about the need for patience and caution when practising magic than any words of mine." He paced up and down a little, considering. "Let us strike a bargain. I will advance your studies so that your energy and curiosity will be well occupied. You will mend your manners (yes, I know all about your spying from behind the door!), will work hard at every task I set, and will always ask me if you want to experiment with a spell. Is it a bargain?"

The apprentice could hardly believe his ears. He had fully expected to be turned into stone, or condemned to begging his bread in the gutter. But here was his dear, good master offering him what he had longed for. "Oh, yes," he whispered. "Yes, indeed, my master. It is most certainly a bargain." And the rays of the rising sun shone on them through the window as they shook hands on the agreement.

A Sprig of Rosemary

Ruth Ainsworth

Joanna had the smallest garden you can possibly imagine. It wasn't really a garden at all – it was a small, paved yard, so small that when the umbrella clothes' drier was hung with clothes, there was barely room to squeeze round it.

But when Joanna's mother was not doing any washing and the clothes' drier was folded together, then the yard – what there was of it – was all Joanna's.

She certainly made the most of it. She could skip if she stayed in one spot, so she stayed in one spot. She collected snails from the walls and tried to persuade them to race across the paving-stones. The winner was rewarded with a bit of cabbage leaf, or the green frond off a carrot.

Her two dolls, Milly and Molly, had tea parties, using the blue, enamel teaset that had been Joanna's mother's, and eating, if they were lucky, some biscuit crumbs and a few raisins. Milly was greedy and had to be scolded for eating more than her share. Molly, on the other hand, was faddy and had to be coaxed.

Joanna's little house was squeezed between two bigger ones. The next door house had a garden shaped like an 'L' which Joanna could look at if she stood on a kitchen chair and looked over the wall. At one of the upper windows, an old lady sat, day in and day out, watching, watching all that Joanna did down below. Occasionally, if it were hot and the window were open at the bottom, she waved a white, lace handkerchief.

Then Joanna waved back and she made the dolls wave too.

The old lady's name was Mrs Raven.

One day, Joanna's mother called her indoors. She was holding a letter in her hand.

"Here's a note from Mrs Raven," said her

mother, "and it's about you. She says she often watches you and wonders if you would care to play in her garden. This is what she says:

"It would give me pleasure to have a child playing in my garden again, where no child has played for many years. Would Joanna care to play there sometimes? Let her slip in whenever she wishes. She may pick any flowers she likes and amuse herself how she pleases. Mr Shaw, the gardener, comes every Tuesday, so she will have to play at home that day.

The side door is unlocked till dusk and she may come and go as she pleases. There is no need to ask. She will always be welcome.

Yours sincerely,
Evelina Raven."

"May I go, mother?"

"Will you like being all alone there?"

"It will be the same as being alone here. I shall be only just through the wall. If you call me, I shall hear. And if I call you, you'll hear, too. May I go now, this very minute?"

"You are in a hurry to get away. Let me brush your hair, and you'd better wash your face, as well."

Joanna never forgot her first day in the next door garden. It was hot and still, and the scent of the flowers was strange and unusual. Mr Shaw was only interested in flowers as there were no cabbages or potatoes anywhere, only some strawberries under nets, and some raspberry canes. There were flowers of every colour and kind. Lilies and little low pansies. Tall sweet peas. White and yellow daisies. Roses and plants that smelled sweetly when crushed between the finger and thumb. But she did not find out about these till later.

At first Joanna dared hardly pick a blade of grass, but she remembered what the letter said and soon ventured to gather a few roses for her mother. Then she collected fragrant leaves to tear up small and mix with water in a glass bottle. This she called: "making scent."

At eleven o'clock each morning – Joanna soon learned to listen for the chiming of the clock – a lady in an overall came through the French window and placed a tray on a stone bench. There was a glass of milk on the tray and two biscuits.

"With Mrs Raven's compliments," said the lady.

Joanna began to look forward to the tray, the biscuits were so delicious. They were home-made, not from a shop. Sometimes they were decorated with cherries, sometimes nuts, sometimes a dab of icing. She ate them slowly, not wasting a crumb. Milly and Molly watched her hungrily.

When Joanna grew used to the next door garden, she began to enjoy herself even more. She no longer started if a branch creaked, or looked over her shoulder if a bird flew out of a bush. She even forgot about Mrs Evelina Raven at her upper window, unless she chanced to look that way and see the flutter of the white handkerchief. Then she waved back and smiled.

The first time she saw the other child was on a sunny day, when the roses were in bloom. She had filled her little basket with fallen petals, and was trying to fix a flower in Milly and Molly's hair.

"You're Japanese dolls now," she said. Then she looked up and saw another girl standing by a tree-trunk, very straight, very thin, wearing a white pinafore. She knew at once it was a pinafore from old-fashioned pictures. The girl had one hand on the bark of the tree, and in the other she was holding a white stick.

Joanna went towards her.

"I'm Joanna and I'm allowed to play here. I live next door."

"I'm Rosemary. I don't know if I'm allowed here or not, but I used to know this garden well."

"Was it your garden?"

"Yes. In a way."

"Either it was or it wasn't," said Joanna. "Like black or white."

"But that's not a distinction to me," said the girl with a smile. "I can't tell the difference between black and white, and never could. Except in dreams," she added.

"Then you must be—" Joanna broke off and a blush spread over her freckles.

"Yes, I am. I'm blind. Quite, quite blind. Didn't you guess?"

"No, I didn't. Your eyes are wide open. I thought blind people had their eyes closed."

"No," said Rosemary, "dead people have their eyes shut. Blind people can have them open."

"Would you like to smell my scent? It's only home-made, so it doesn't smell like real perfume."

"Yes, I would." Rosemary sniffed delicately and said, as she sniffed: "I smell balm and thyme and cotton lavender. And I think basil."

"I don't know if you're right or wrong, because I don't know the names of most of the things I picked. You know all about the garden and its plants. How did you learn, without seeing them?"

"I had a wonderful mother," said Rosemary, "who made this garden for me and planted every sweet-smelling herb she could find. She took me round the garden every day and I touched and smelled them all. In the end, I knew them as well as I knew my own bedroom. It seemed to me they were different at different times of the day. Specially fresh in the early morning. Stronger at noon. Best of all in the evening. I've wandered round the garden in the moonlight in my nightgown, breathing it in."

"You must have looked like a ghost," said Joanna.

"Why do you say that?" Rosemary's fingers gripped her arm, and she sounded startled. "Why do you say that word?"

"I didn't mean to upset you. I just meant that anyone in a white nightgown, wandering about in a garden in the moonlight, would look ghostly. That's all I meant."

"Yes, I understand," said Rosemary. "But I must go now. I'll come again tomorrow. Goodbye, Joanna."

"Goodbye." Joanna watched her intently, but lost sight of her among the greenery. Her white pinafore glimmered and faded, like a fade-out in a film.

The next day, when Joanna arrived in the garden, Rosemary was there already.

"I've been round very carefully," said Rosemary, "and there's not a sprig of my name plant anywhere. And there was once. I'll show you where it used to grow."

Rosemary took her hand ("how cold her fingers are," thought Joanna) and with the outstretched white cane in the other, she led her unhesitatingly to a circle of crazy-paving bordered with plants.

"Here's the cotton lavender. Here's where it ought to be, between the lavender and the bergamot. I suppose it died. But no one told me. I should have guessed as it's my name flower. 'Rosemary for remembrance', Mother used to say."

"Would it help me to remember my lessons?" asked Joanna. "That would be useful. We have to learn a list of spellings and be tested on Tuesdays. It makes me hate Tuesdays," she added.

"I don't think rosemary could help you to learn spellings. It might help you to remember something you once knew."

"That doesn't sound so useful," said Joanna doubtfully. "Most of the important things seem to be happening now. Perhaps it's different when you're older."

"It's different for me," said Rosemary. "All my important things happened in the past. Except, of course, meeting you," she added gently. "That's very important."

Sometimes Joanna forgot that Rosemary couldn't see, she joined so easily in any game that Joanna suggested. They often played with the dolls, and Milly and Molly led a more adventurous life than they had up till now. They became famous explorers, and had narrow escapes at least twice a day. They were threatened by crocodiles – poisoned arrows – quicksands – hostile tribes – snake bites.

Rosemary was just as good in less thrilling roles, such as a doctor when Milly and Molly caught the measles, a schoolmistress when they went to school, and a ring-master when they joined the circus.

"I never guessed you were blind at the beginning," said Joanna one day. "And I often forget you are now."

"Didn't you see my white stick? All blind people carry a white stick."

"Yes, but somehow – it didn't mean you

were blind. It seemed more like a wand. A magician's wand. It still does."

"It's almost like a wand to me," admitted Rosemary, "because I have freedom to explore when it's in my hand. I'm lost without it."

While the friendship between the two girls grew closer and warmer, Joanna didn't talk about her new friend to her mother, though she usually told her everything, as naturally as breathing. She realized, soon after their first meeting, that she wanted to keep Rosemary a secret. It had happened in the early days, when her mother had said to her: "I saw you from the bedroom window this morning. You were talking to yourself, and laughing. It looked queer."

"It wasn't queer, Mother, I was talking to Rosemary, and she often makes me laugh."

"Rosemary who?" asked her mother quickly.

"Oh, I don't know her other name. I don't know even if she's got another name. She's just someone very very nice I play with."

Her mother seemed relieved. "Oh, an imaginary friend. You used to have them when you were younger. Aren't you out-growing these pretend people?"

"I'm not outgrowing Rosemary. She's older than me, or I think she is, and very sensible. You'd approve." That was the only time she had ever mentioned Rosemary to anyone.

Rosemary had a habit of disappearing when the tray with the milk and biscuits was laid on the stone seat. She vanished among the bushes, without a leaf stirring or a twig cracking. She never reappeared till the tray was removed.

At first, Joanna saved a biscuit for her, but she so plainly didn't want it, though she refused politely.

"Eat it yourself," she said. "I've outgrown biscuits."

"I shall never outgrow these biscuits," said Joanna, licking the icing off with her tongue before she took her first half-moon bite. "They are my favourite."

The only cloud in Rosemary's clear sky was the absence of the rosemary bush. Never a day passed without her lingering by the cotton lavender and the bergamot, feeling with her free hand, and bending to smell, but all in vain.

"It worries you, doesn't it?" said Joanna sympathetically. "It not being there, I mean."

"Yes it does. If I could smell it again, and touch it, I'm sure I could remember something I've forgotten."

"Supposing it's something sad?" said Joanna.

"I want to remember it anyhow, sad or happy. It's part of me. I want to be complete. You're not a whole person if your memory has a gap in it."

Joanna made up her mind she would somehow get hold of a rosemary bush and ask Mr Shaw, the gardener, to plant it in place of the old one. But how? She had no idea how to begin. But where there's a will there's a way. She decided to ask help from her father, who would be less likely to ask awkward questions than her mother.

"Daddy, will you please buy me a rosemary bush? Quite a tiny baby one will do. It'll grow."

"It won't grow in *this* garden," said her

father, firmly. "Just a waste of money."

He put his pipe back in his mouth, and opened the paper.

"I don't want it for this garden. I'm not as silly as all that!" said Joanna. "No, I want it for Mrs Raven's garden, where I go and play."

"She's rich enough to buy her own rosemary bushes," said her father, "but she's been very kind to you, I must say. All right, I'll see what I can do."

Joanna heaved a sigh of relief. No awkward questions. No cross-examination. Just that re-assuring: "I'll see what I can do."

A few days later, her father gave her something soggy, wrapped up in newspaper.

"I got this from a chap at work," he said. "He's a great gardener. Says it's the wrong time of year for it to strike, but they're unpredictable things. I said I'd like it, right or wrong time. Is that OK?"

"Daddy, you're an angel. I'll take it across for Mr Shaw to plant now. It's Tuesday, so he'll be there."

She ran out of the house and through the side door. Mr Shaw was putting his tools away. He was a gruff, whiskery old man, with red-rimmed eyes. She was rather frightened of him.

"Please, Mr Shaw, will you plant this rosemary for me? It might live. Anyhow, it's got a better chance of living if *you* plant it. I'll show you the place."

She indicated the place between the cotton lavender and the bergamot and fled, her heart pounding.

"That's a queer little lass," said Mr Shaw to himself, taking a hand fork out of the shed. "But I'll do what she asks for the sake of that other one. She reminds me of her, in a way. Same clear voice and light step like a bird."

The next day Joanna visited the garden early. There was the rosemary, with its spiky, dark green leaves, looking hearty, firmed down in the wet soil. Mr Shaw had done his work well. A few minutes later, Rosemary joined her, silently, as always.

"Rosemary, can you see – I mean smell – do you notice anything different just here?"

The white stick inched along like an exploring finger. Then its owner bent down.

"It's rosemary. A little young rosemary. Oh Joanna, how kind of you. I've longed for one for ages."

She pinched a sprig and smelt her fingers. She broke off a leaf and bit it delicately. Her face was transfigured – but was it extreme pleasure or extreme pain? Joanna took her hand in hers. It was colder than ever. Then Rosemary began speaking: "Now I remember. It all comes back. I was walking along a cliff path with Mother. There was so much to smell and enjoy and hear. The bees on the flowers, the gulls crying overhead. It was a lovely spot because it had once been a garden – only it had been neglected for years and years and gone wild. But some of the garden flowers lived on among the wild ones, among the gorse bushes and the wild thyme and the clover. Then, I was sure I smelt rosemary. Perhaps I trod on it and bruised it with my foot. I stepped aside and bent down to pick a sprig – and the cliff crumbled away. Someone screamed louder than the seagulls – and I fell down, down, down. But I never reached the bottom. Sometimes I think I'm falling still, as one does in a dream."

That morning the tray was not brought out and neither was Mrs Raven at her window. She hadn't been there for several days. When the clock had finished chiming eleven, Joanna looked in vain at the French door, and then raised her eyes to the bedroom window. Mrs Raven had come back. She was not sitting in her chair, as usual, but was standing up and leaning out, waving her lace handkerchief.

Joanna waved back.

"It's Mrs Raven," she said to Rosemary. "I haven't seen her lately."

Rosemary turned her face upward, her dark eyes not blank and wandering, but bright with recognition.

"Mother! Mother!" she cried. "Mother, I'm coming!"

Joanna felt the thin, cold fingers slip from her grasp and at the same time she saw the figure of Mrs Raven fade from the window. Then the garden was emptier and quieter than she had ever known it. The friendly ghost, whom she had learned to love, had joined that other ghost who had been waiting for her. She ran home, bewildered and upset, trying to understand.

That evening, the letter-box clicked and her mother picked an envelope off the mat. She opened it and read aloud:

"It's from Mrs Raven's housekeeper," she said.

"I am writing to tell you that Mrs Raven died suddenly this morning, at eleven o'clock. She was a kind mistress and I shall miss her. She often said what pleasure it gave her to see your little girl playing in the garden. Her own little girl died at about the same age, through a tragic accident."

"Well, we never know what's round the corner," said her mother. "Here today, gone tomorrow. When did you see Mrs Raven last, Joanna? You told me she often waved to you."

"Some time ago," said Joanna. But she thought to herself; "Only this morning. Only this morning at eleven."

The house next door was sold and the new people built an extension into the garden. A studio, it was thought. They gave parties there. They made the wall higher which darkened Joanna's tiny yard even more.

Joanna grew old enough to go alone to the local park and play with her friends. Her mother was pleased that she no longer talked to herself or had make-believe companions. Later still, when she studied Hamlet at school, she came across Ophelia's lines:

"Rosemary, that's for remembrance."

"But I don't need rosemary to help me to remember," she said to herself. "I shall never forget. Never in my life."

A is for Aaargh!

Frank Rodgers

"This is Miss Snitchell," said the headmistress to Class Three. "She will be taking you while your own teacher is off ill." She turned to Miss Snitchell and whispered, "I'm afraid this is the worst class in the school."

"Don't worry," whispered Miss Snitchell, "I know how to deal with rascals."

The headmistress left and "Beasty" Barrett, the class bully, grinned and nudged his nasty pal, "Biff" Higson. "Let's have some fun with this one," he whispered. The others heard this and giggled. This could be fun, they thought!

Miss Snitchell cleared her throat. "Now, children," she began . . . "we'll start with an alphabet exercise to test your vocabulary."

Beasty turned to Biff and winked. "She thinks we're babies," he said. "She's a push-over!"

"Who will give me an example to begin with?" said Miss Snitchell, looking round brightly. "A is for . . . ?"

"AAAAAAARGH!" gurgled Beasty, falling backwards, a plastic arrow sticking out of his head.

The class roared with laughter. Beasty was up to his tricks again! Miss Snitchell smiled faintly. She could take a joke.

"Remove your arrow, boy, and put it away," she said when the laughter subsided. Miss Snitchell looked around and continued. "B is for . . . ?" she said.

"Boo!" yelled Biff, jumping up from his seat.

"Sit down, child!" said Miss Snitchell sternly. Biff sat down, grinning smugly. Miss Snitchell shook her finger at him and carried on. "C is for centipede," she said quickly before she could be interrupted.

"That's right, Miss," shouted Beasty, "C is for centipede . . . which is a creepy-crawly like my pet spider!"

Beasty set his spider free on the desk-top. Everyone shrieked as the spider scuttled down a chair leg and set off across the floor, but much to Beasty's disappointment his hairy little pet disappeared down a crack in the floorboards.

"Now, sit down and pay attention," called Miss Snitchell, "please!"

The children sat down and smiled. This was good fun! When everything was quiet Miss Snitchell began again.

"D is for deplorable," said Miss Snitchell sharply, pointing at Beasty, "which is what your behaviour has been, young man!" Beasty smiled angelically. The class tittered. "Now," smiled Miss Snitchell, the class quiet once more, "we will continue."

"E is for . . . EEEEEK!" she shrieked as a mouse ran along the floor and jumped on to one of her shoes. Biff Higson, amid screams of laughter from the class, ran over and picked it up.

"Sorry, Miss," he said, grinning, as he put it in his pocket. "It's my pet mouse, Mickey. He escaped."

Miss Snitchell rapped on the desk for silence. She looked quite stern. "F is for fright, which is what I got from your pet mouse, my boy." The class laughed. Miss Snitchell continued. "G is for grandmother, which is what I am. I have two handsome grandsons, about your age. They are the top goalscorers with their school team. Here is a picture of them holding the Schools Championship Cup."

The boys were impressed and the girls smiled. But Biff glowered at Beasty. "She's better than I thought," he muttered.

"Just wait," hissed Beasty, "we haven't finished with her yet!"

"Now," said Miss Snitchell, "back to the alphabet. H is for?"

"Handsome," said good-looking Jim Peters from the back. The other boys rolled their eyes and the girls smiled.

"Good," said Miss Snitchell.

"H is for horror!" grinned Beasty. "I love horror films!"

"Do you, now?" said Miss Snitchell. "Do you really . . . ?" She trailed off and looked at

164

Beasty in an odd way. Beasty grinned and nodded his head.

Miss Snitchell continued. "I is for . . . ?"

"ICKYPOO!" sniggered Biff loudly. The class giggled.

"That's enough!" snapped Miss Snitchell. "J is for jungle and jack-in-the-box and juggernaut. K is for . . . ?"

"KING KONG!" bellowed Beasty, lumbering down the aisle like an ape. The class laughed again, encouraging Beasty and Biff.

"L is for Leopard-Man!" snarled Biff, growling and clawing at the girls. "And M is for Monster movies!"

"Yeah . . . M is for Mummy!" shouted Beasty, winding a scarf round his face. "The Mummy from the Tomb!" he wailed, walking about stiffly.

"N is for nasty!" yelled Biff, throwing his book in the air.

The class was now in uproar. Miss Snitchell shouted but her voice couldn't be heard.

"O is for 'orrible! Like what I am!" yelled Beasty gleefully, jumping on top of a desk.

From there he controlled the class just like the conductor of an orchestra. He raised his hand. "P is for . . . ?"

"PUTRID!" yelled the class.

"Q is for . . . ?"

"QUICKSAND!" they shouted.

"R is for . . . ?"

"ROTTEN!"

"S is for . . . ?"

"SLIME!"

"T is for . . . ?"

"TERRIFIED!"

Miss Snitchell seemed to give up. She slumped forward on her desk. The class looked at her curiously, with evil little grins. They wanted Miss Snitchell to watch them. It would be no fun if she didn't. They were so enjoying themselves! A muffled sound came from the teacher's desk.

"Heh, heh, she's cracked!" grinned Beasty.

They gathered round her desk and listened to Miss Snitchell as she spoke into her arms. "U is for . . ." she whispered.

"Louder, Miss!" they shouted gleefully. "We can't hear you, Miss!" They listened again.

"U . . ." said Miss Snitchell, her voice slightly muffled by her arms, "is for . . . UUUUUUUUURRGH!"

The class were startled. Uuuurrgh? Was that a word? Puzzled, they looked at each other. Miss Snitchell was going on, her voice growing stronger and louder.

"V is for VAMPIRE!"

The class looked at one another.

"Ha, ha," said Beasty, "Miss Snitchell got the joke!"

The class started to laugh but stopped suddenly as Miss Snitchell raised her head.

"W," she said, "is for WEREWOLF!!"

The class gasped – the game was definitely over.

Miss Snitchell had changed. Her little bird-like face was hairy and had a pointed nose, ears and dripping fangs . . .

Miss Snitchell *was* a Werewolf! Couldn't she take a joke?

But Miss Snitchell didn't look at all in the mood for laughs. She rose slowly, her red eyes blazing. "X is for my signature," she hissed, and scratched a big X on the blackboard with

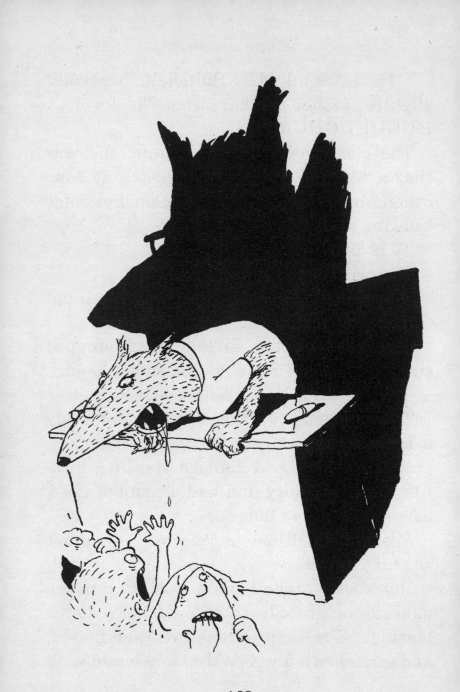

one of her long, sharp, black nails. SCREEEEEEEEEEEEEK!! The class moaned.

Miss Snitchell's eyes narrowed. "Y is for Yeti," she snarled, holding up a snapshot. "My hairy monster friend from the Himalayas." The class stared open-mouthed, goggle-eyed. Beasty and Biff turned a lovely shade of green as Miss Snitchell's hairy finger pointed at them, and then to the rest of the class.

"And finally," she growled, "Z is for Zombie! And all of you will be as watchful as zombies when I teach you from now on. Do you understand?"

The class gulped and nodded together. They understood.

"Now," said Miss Snitchell, "as you all seem to be fond of monsters and horror stories, each of you can write out an alphabet for me for tomorrow morning . . . a HORRIBLE alphabet, staring with A is for Aaargh!"

She grinned wickedly at Biff and Beasty who slid down in their seats. The interval bell rang but nobody moved. Miss Snitchell lifted up her hairy snout and gave a long, piercing, triumphant howl.

Just then the headmistress came in.

The class looked at the headmistress.

The headmistress looked at Miss Snitchell, then at the class.

Miss Snitchell smiled sweetly.

"I'm pleased to see that Class Three behaved themselves, Miss Snitchell," said the headmistress.

"Oh, yes," said Miss Snitchell, "they were little angels." She turned to the class and her eyes twinkled mischievously.

"Class dismissed," she said.

ACKNOWLEDGEMENTS

The publishers wish to thank the following for permission to reproduce copyright material. All possible care has been taken to trace the ownership of every story included and to make full acknowledgements for its use. If any errors have accidentally occurred, they will be corrected in subsequent editions, provided notification is sent to the publishers.

Colin Thompson: "The Haunted Suitcase" from *The Haunted Suitcase and other stories* by Colin Thompson; first published 1996 by Hodder Children's Books and reproduced with their permission.

Bel Mooney: "I'm Scared'" from *I'm Scared* by Bel Mooney; first published by Mammoth. Reproduced by permission of David Higham Associates.

Amabel Williams-Ellis: "The Great White Cat" from *The Enchanted World* by Amabel Williams-Ellis; first published 1950 by Hodder & Stoughton Ltd. Reproduced by permission of Hodder Children's Books.

Michael Rosen: "Gobbleguts" and "Cherry-Berry" from *Clever Cakes* by Michael Rosen; published by Walker Books. Text copyright © 1991 Michael Rosen, illustrated by Caroline Holden. Reproduced by permission of Walker Books Ltd.

Rose Impey: *The Flat Man*. Text copyright © Rose Impey 1988. *The Flat Man* is reproduced with the kind permission of Mathew Price Ltd, The Old Glove Factory, Bristol Road, Sherborne, Dorset, and is one of the *Creepies* series published by HarperCollins. Canadian rights by permission of Carolrhoda Books, Inc.

Mary Danby: "Jumo and the Giraffe" from *Animal Ghosts*, edited by Carolyn Lloyd; first published by Collins, 1971. Copyright © Mary Danby, 1971. Reprinted by permission of the author.

Jamie Rix: "School Dinners" from *Ghostly Tales for Ghastly Kids* by Jamie Rix; first published by André Deutsch Ltd and copyright © Jamie Rix 1992. Reproduced by permission of Eunice McMullen Children's Literary Agent Ltd.

David Parker: "Ponkyfoot" from *All the Year Round*, edited by Shona McEller; first published by Evans Brothers, 1980.

Catherine Storr: "Finn's Mistake" from *Finn's Animals* by Catherine Storr; first published by William Heinemann Ltd and reproduced by permission of Reed Consumer Books Ltd.

Funny stories

for 5 year olds

Chosen by Helen Paiba

A bright and varied selection of wonderfully
entertaining stories by some of the very
best writers for children. Perfect for
reading alone or aloud – and for dipping into
time and time again. With stories from
Dick King-Smith, Tony Ross, Alf Prøysen,
Malorie Blackman and many more,
this book will provide hours of fantastic fun.

Funny stories

for 6 year olds

Chosen by Helen Paiba

A bright and varied selection of wonderfully
entertaining stories by some of the very
best writers for children. Perfect for
reading alone or aloud – and for dipping
into time and time again. With stories from
Margaret Mahy, David Henry Wilson, Francesca
Simon, Tony Bradman and many more,
this book will provide hours of fantastic fun.

Funny stories

for 7 Year Olds

Chosen by Helen Paiba

A bright and varied selection of wonderfully entertaining stories by some of the very best writers for children. Perfect for reading alone or aloud – and for dipping into time and time again. With stories from Dick King-Smith, Michael Bond, Philippa Gregory, Jacqueline Wilson and many more, this book will provide hours of fantastic fun.

Funny Stories

for 8 year olds

Chosen by Helen Paiba

A bright and varied selection of wonderfully entertaining stories by some of the very best writers for children. Perfect for reading alone or aloud – and for dipping into time and time again. With stories from Judy Blume, Anne Fine, Dick King-Smith, Morris Gleitzman and many more, this book will provide hours of fantastic fun.

Tom Percival

Little Legends

THE SPELL THIEF

Welcome to
Tale Town!

Life for Jack is great — he's got a magical talking hen called Betsy, he lives in a town where stories *literally* grow on trees, and all his best friends live there with him. That is, until new kid in town, Anansi, arrives . . .

When Jack sees Anansi having a secret meeting with a troll — *everything* changes. Trolls mean trouble and Jack will stop at *nothing* to prove that Tale Town is in danger. Even if that means using stolen magic!

They may be small, but their adventures are epic!

Little Legends are also available from

Me Books

ELLI WOOLLARD
Swashbuckle Lil

The Secret Pirate

Two brilliantly
illustrated rhyming
stories!

ILLUSTRATED BY LAURA ELLEN ANDERSON

Lil is a pirate, a good sort of pirate,
And when there is someone to save,
She'll do what is right (if it takes her all night).
Yes, she'll always be bold and be brave.

When evil pirate Stinkbeard tries to kidnap Lil's teacher, it's
up to schoolgirl and secret pirate, Lil, to come to the rescue.

In story two it's sports day, but there's a very hungry croc
on the loose. Can Lil and her trusty parrot, Carrot,
scare Stinkbeard and his pet croc away?